DAYDREAMS

Coloring book illustrated by Hanna Karlzon

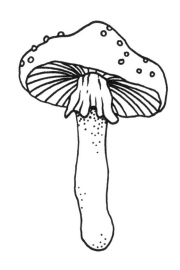

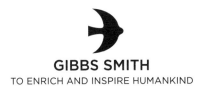

GIBBS SMITH
TO ENRICH AND INSPIRE HUMANKIND

25 24 23 22   13 12 11 10
Daydreams Coloring Book
Illustrations © 2016 Hanna Karlzon.

Swedish edition copyright © 2015 Pagina Förlags AB, Sweden.
All rights reserved.

Gibbs Smith
P.O. Box 667
Layton, Utah 84041

1.800.835.4993 orders
www.gibbs-smith.com

ISBN: 978-1-4236-4556-6

Also available! *Daydreams* postcards
to color and send to your friends.

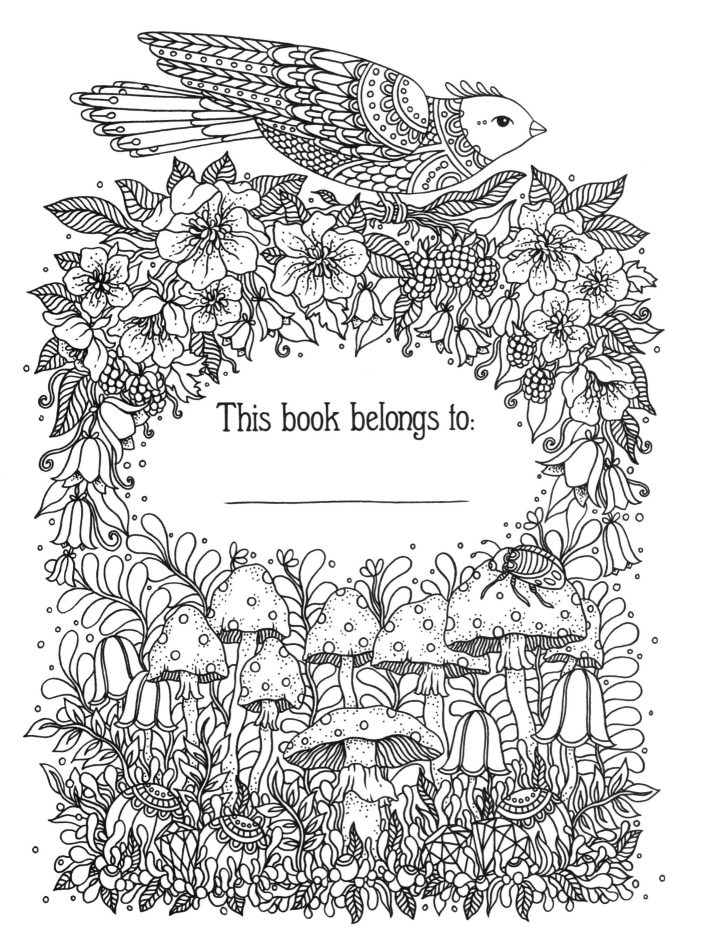

This book belongs to:

_____

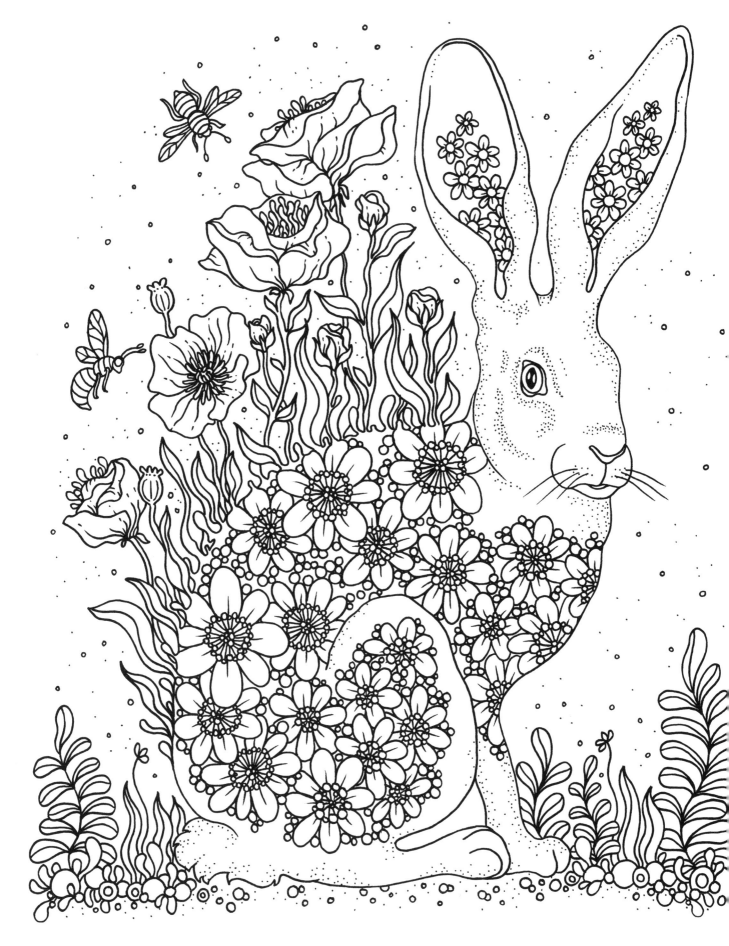

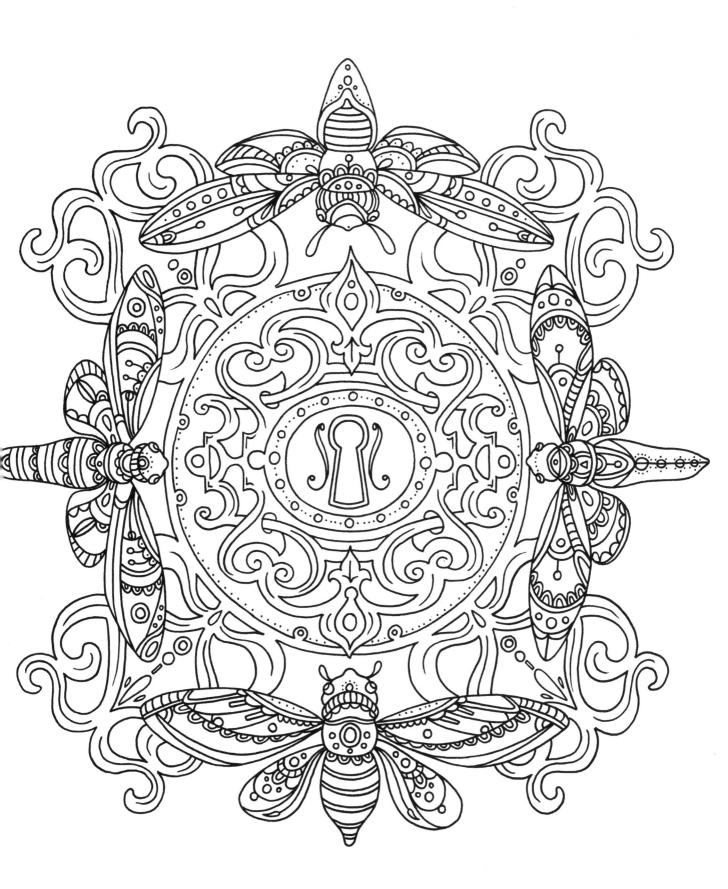

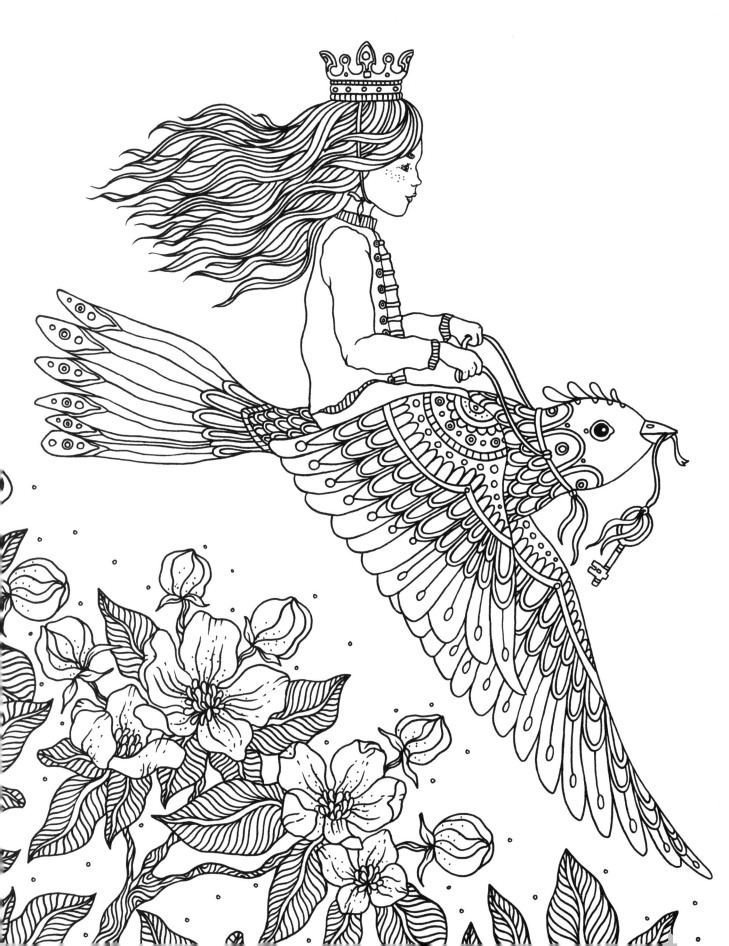

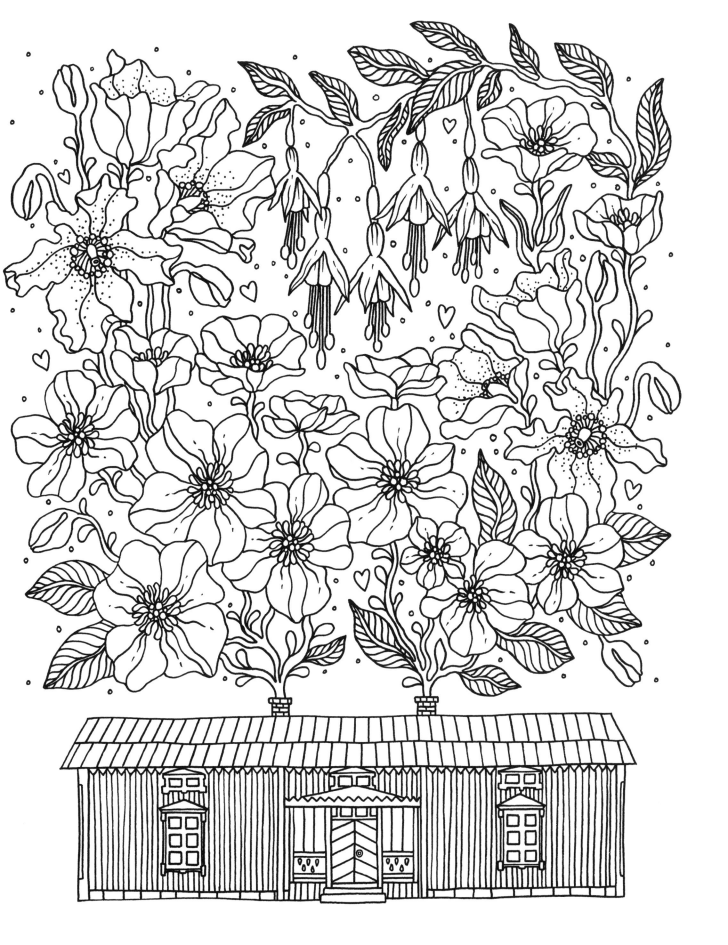

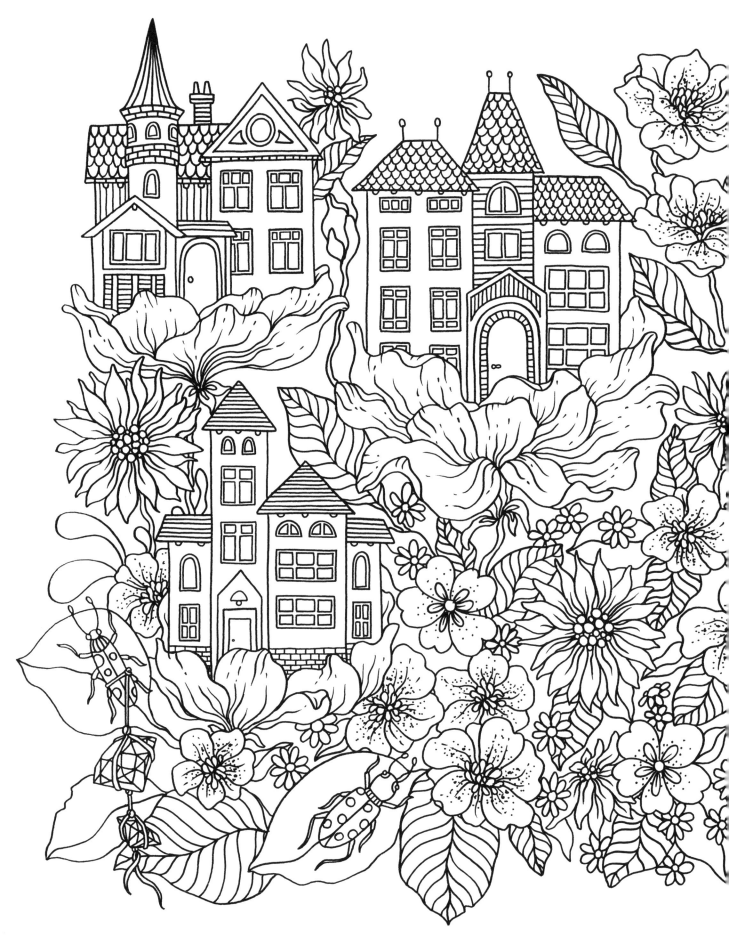

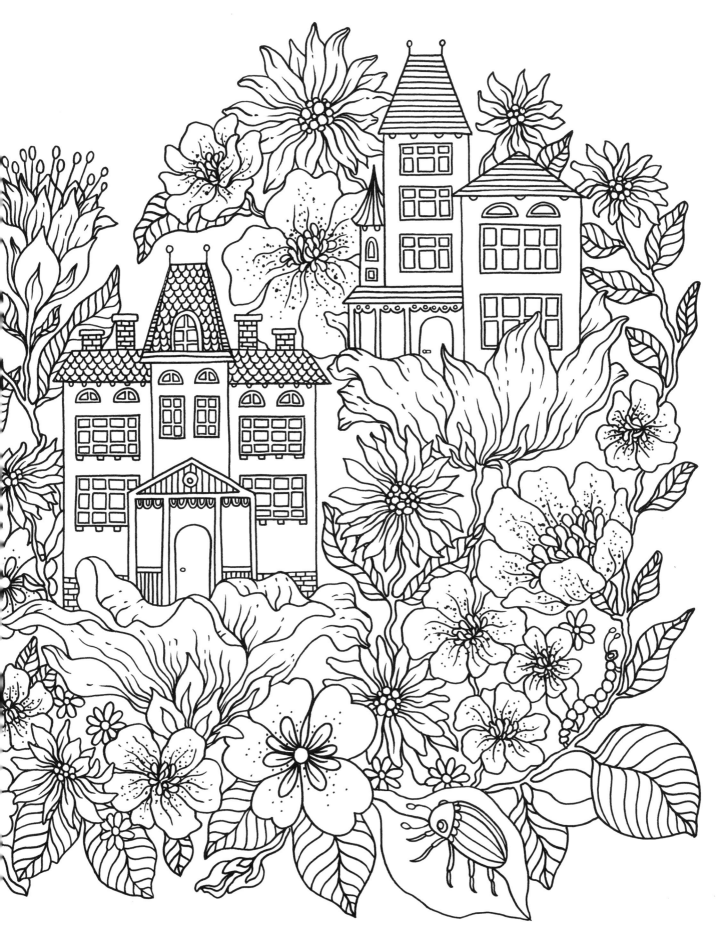

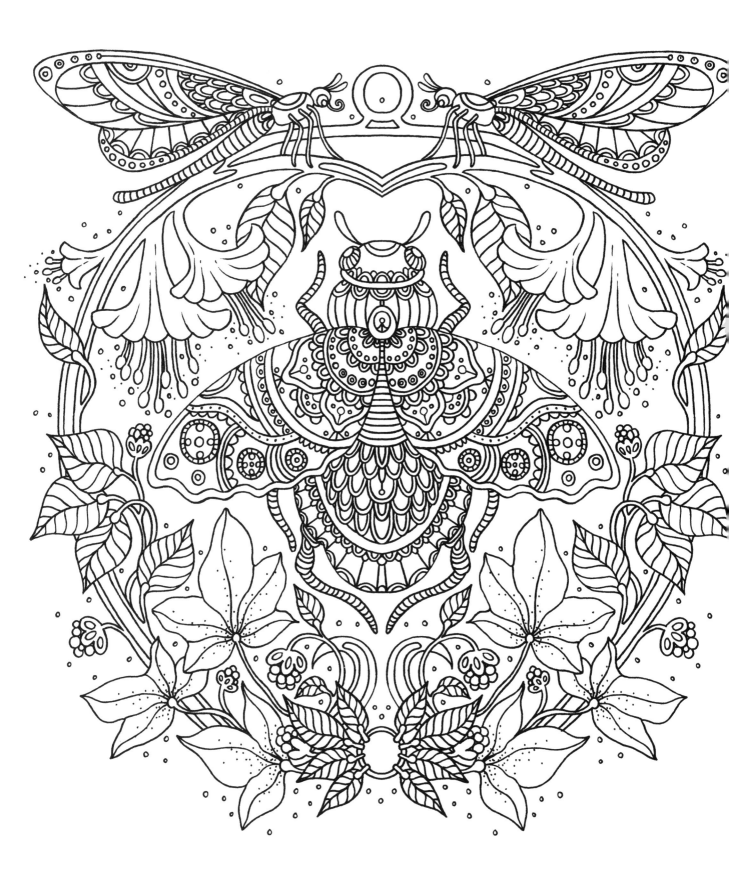

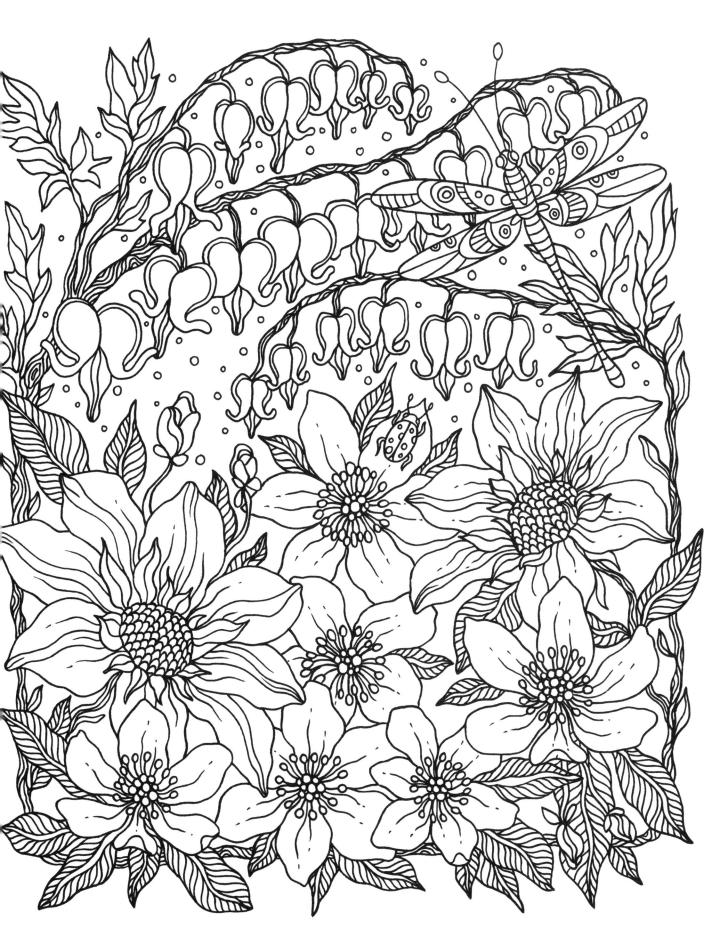

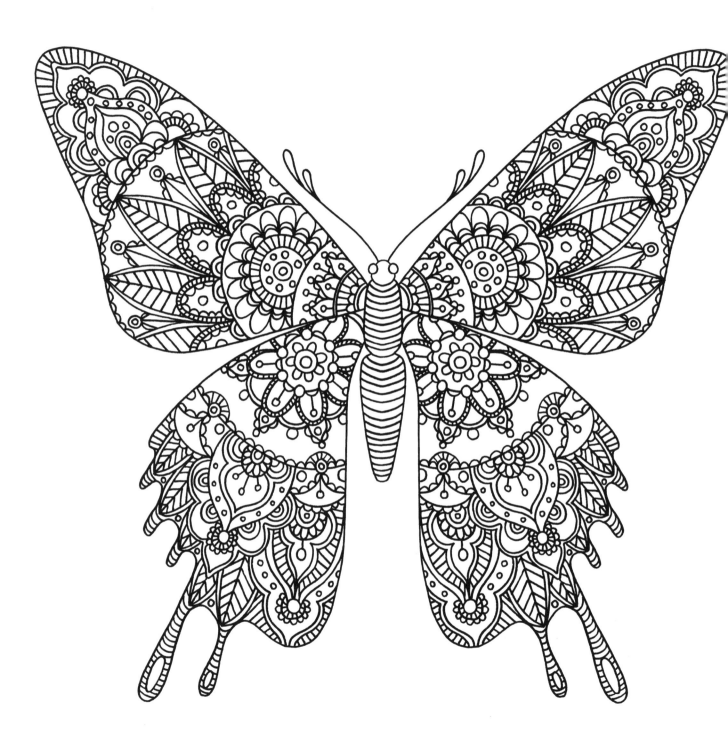

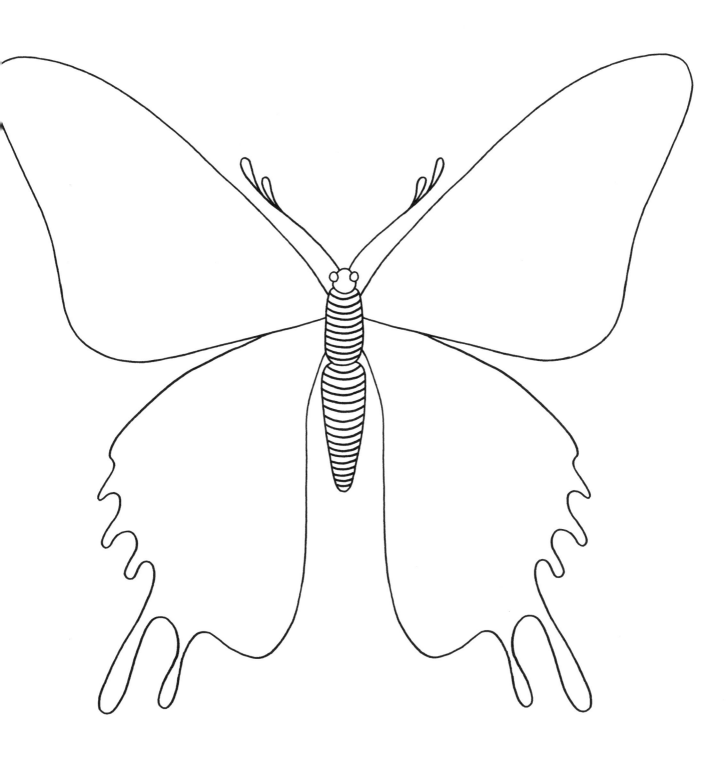

Draw your own patterns on this butterfly.

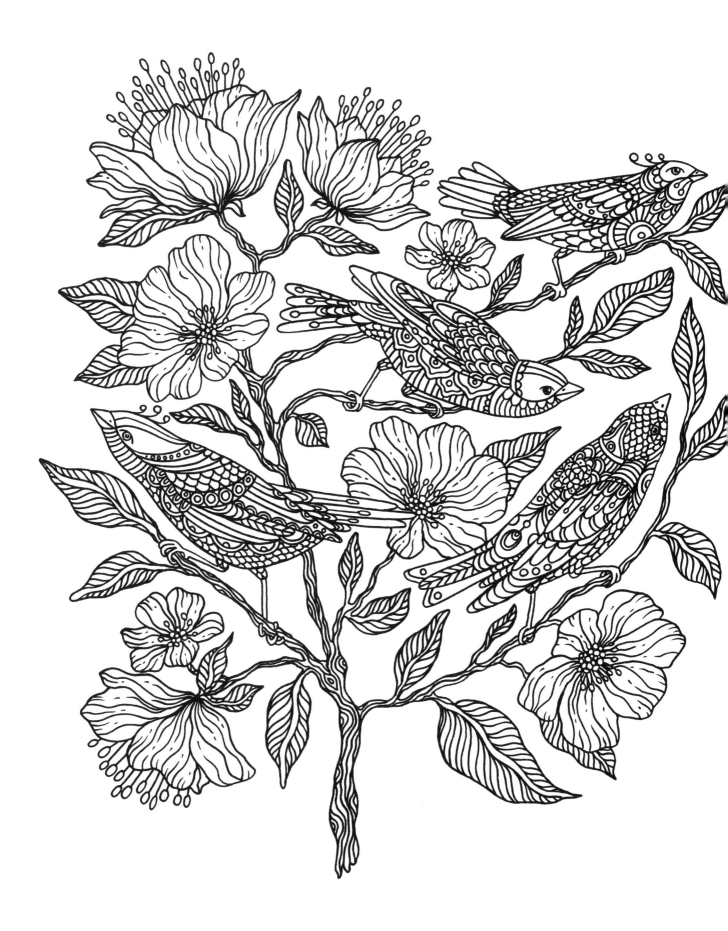

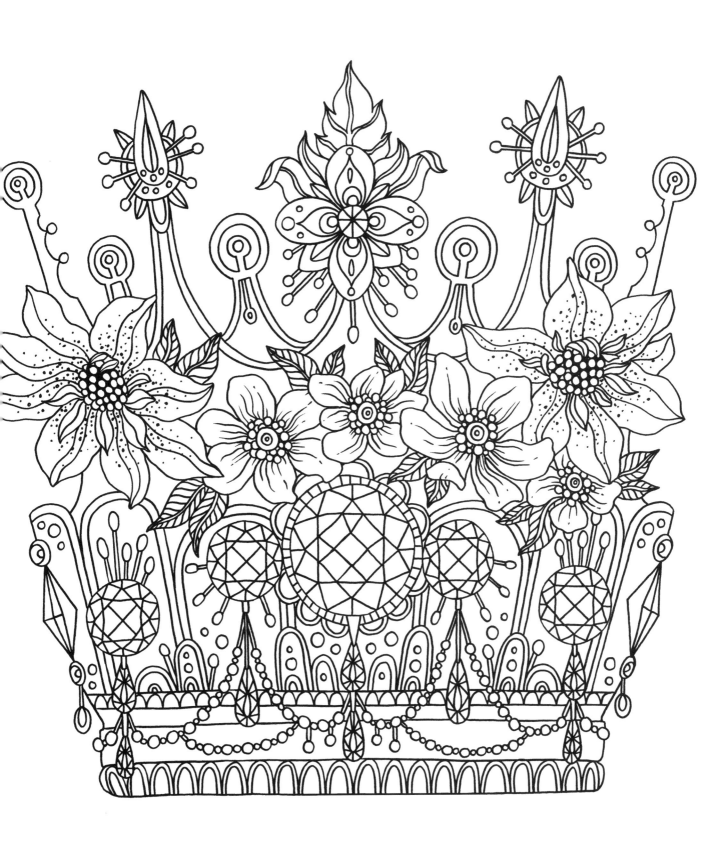

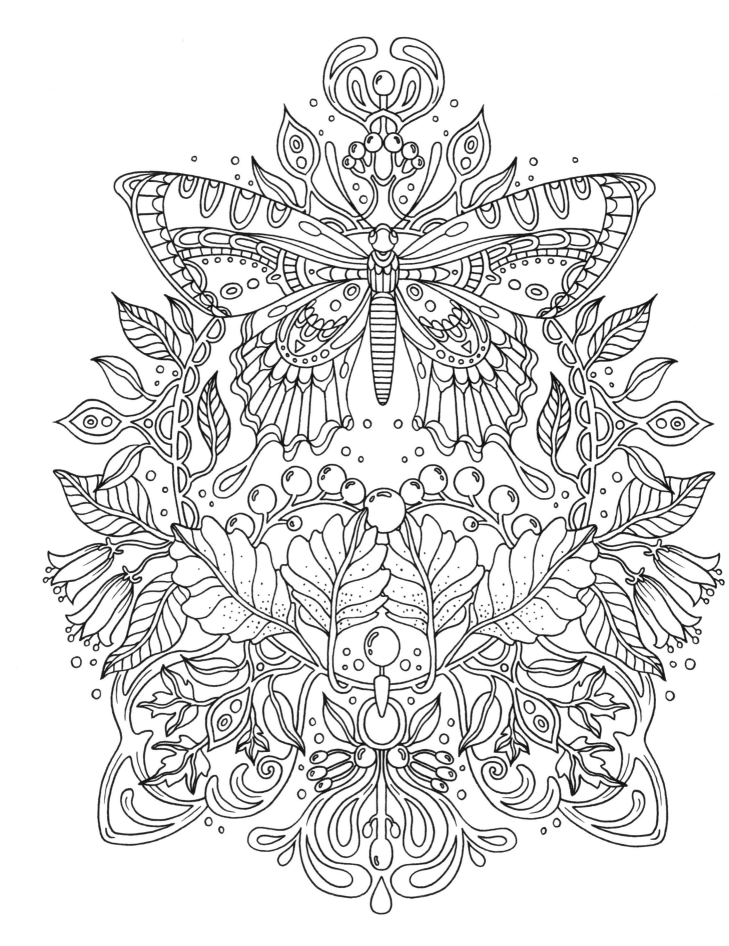

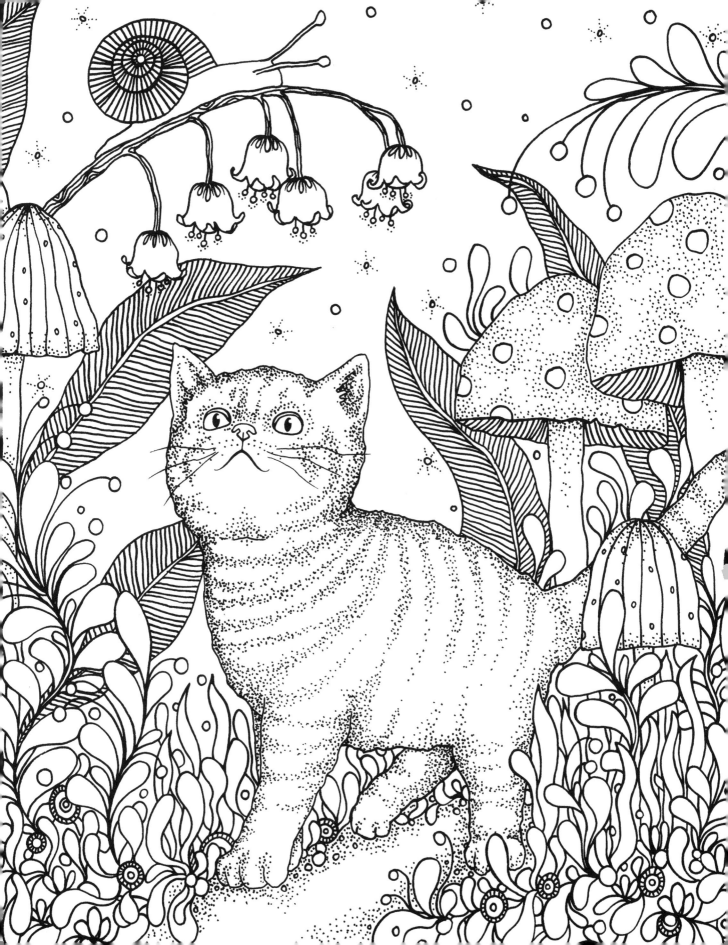

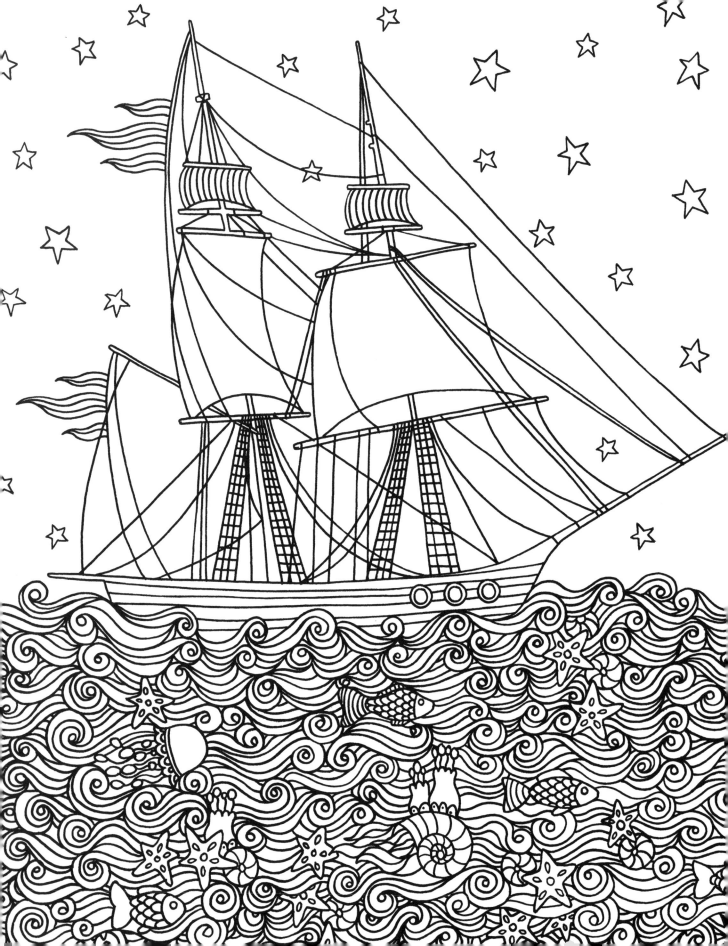

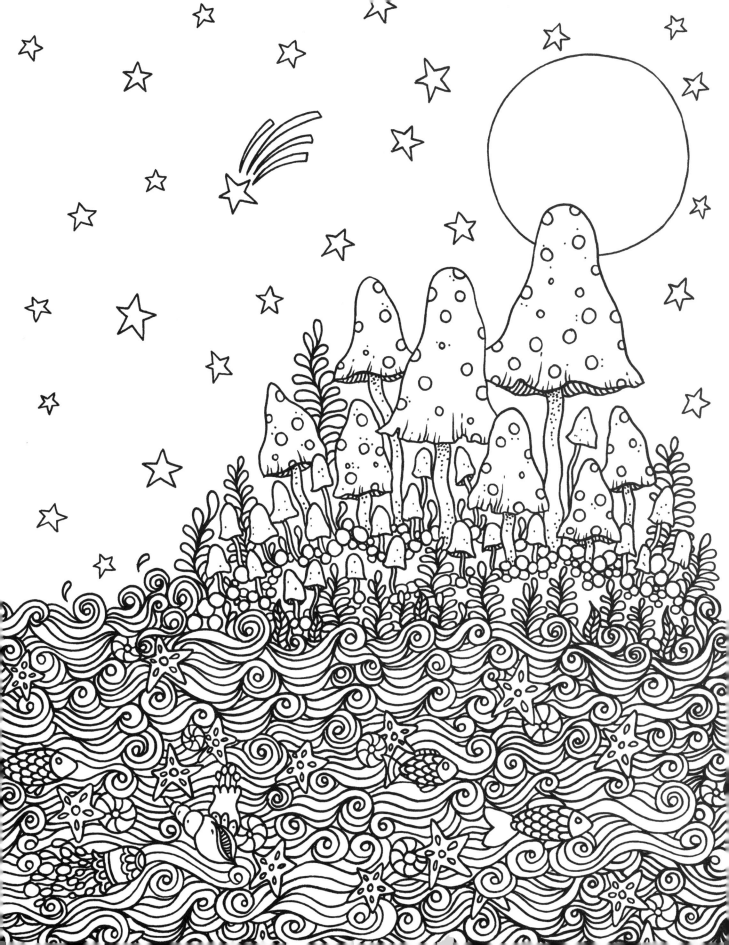

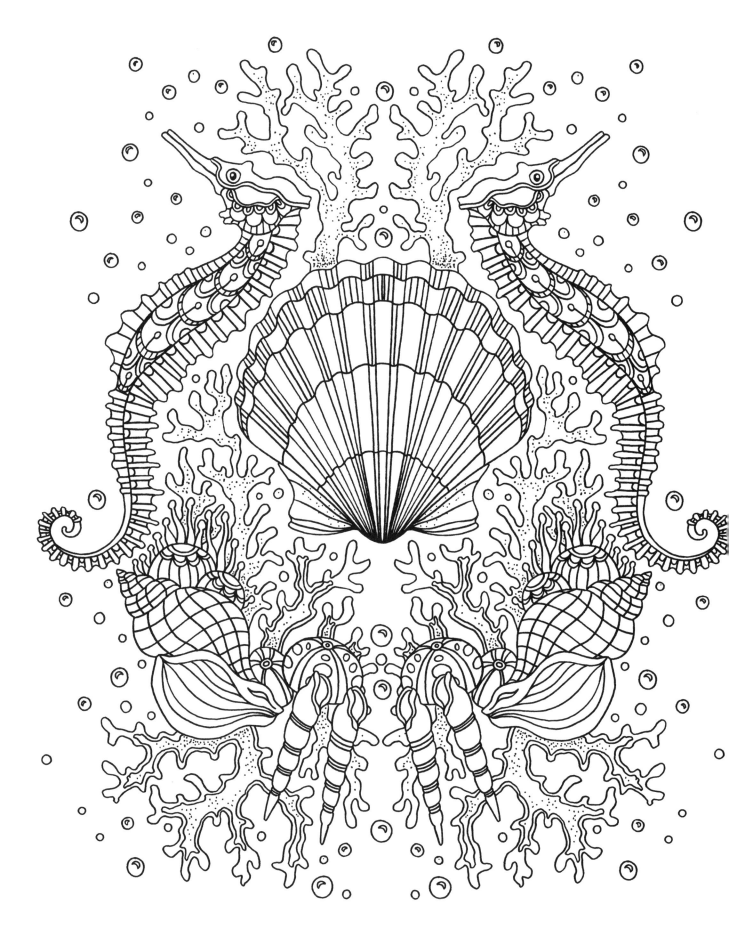

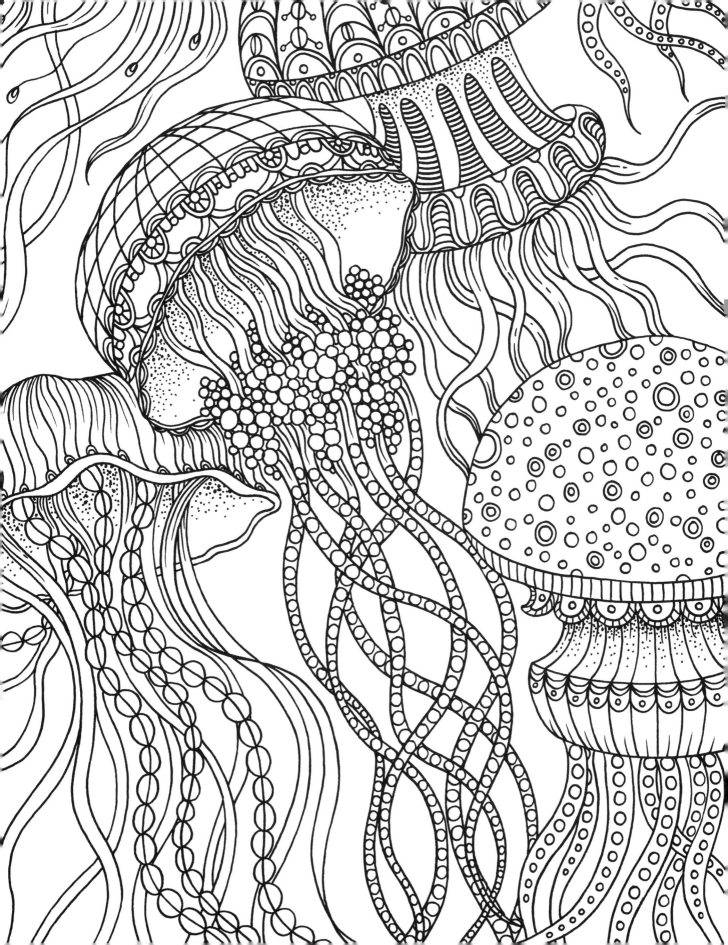

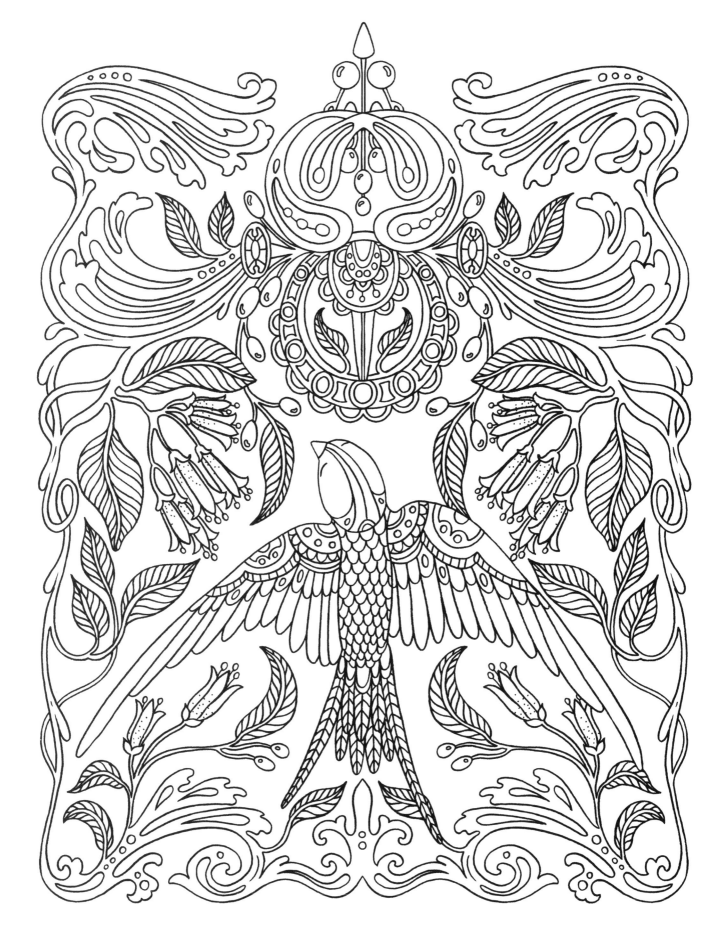

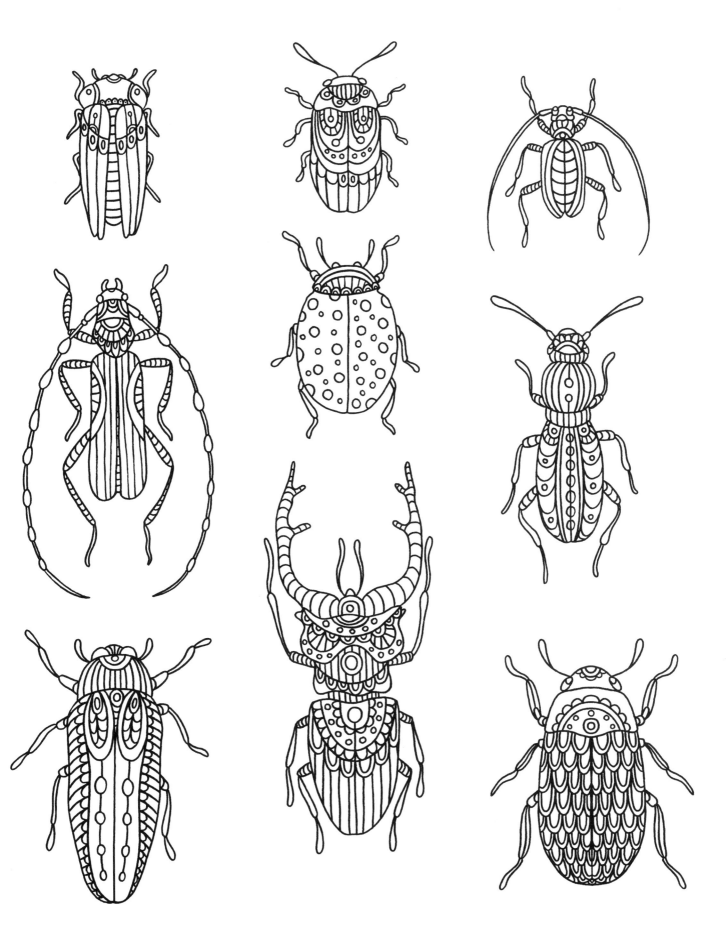

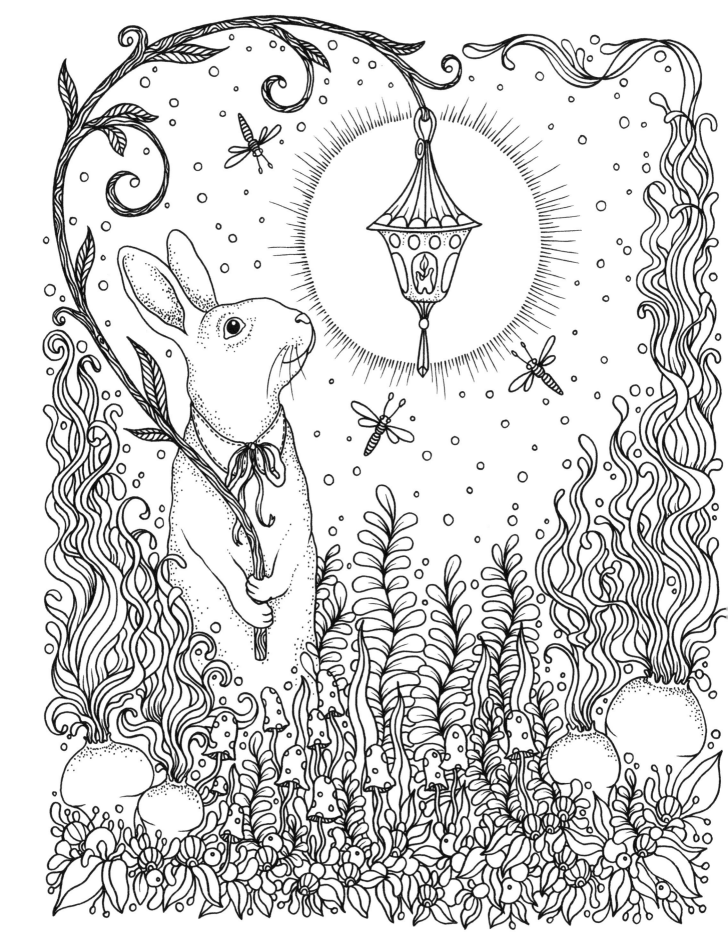

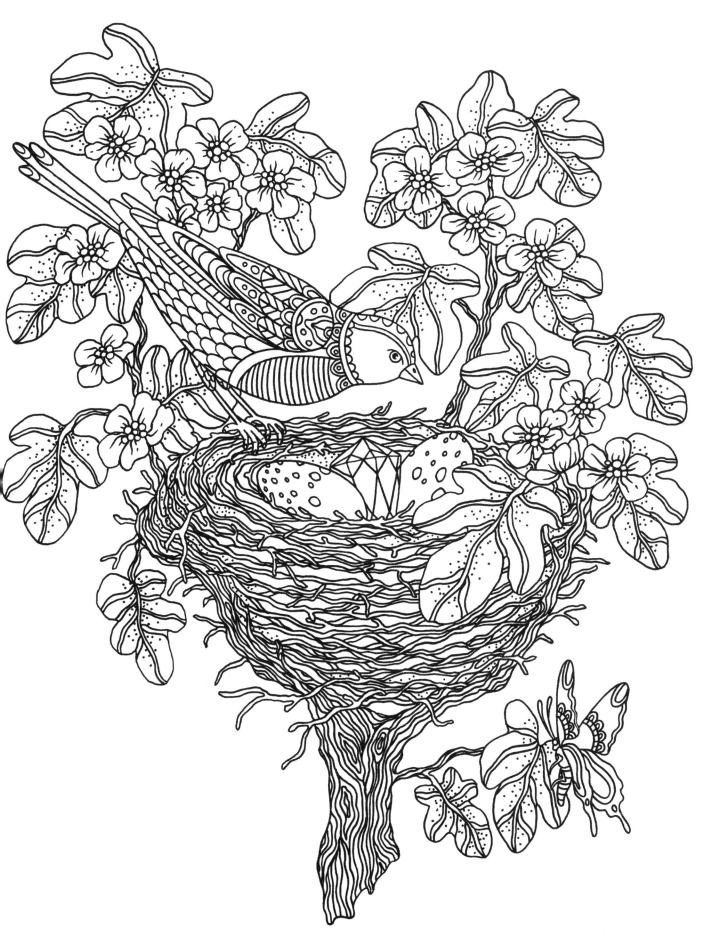

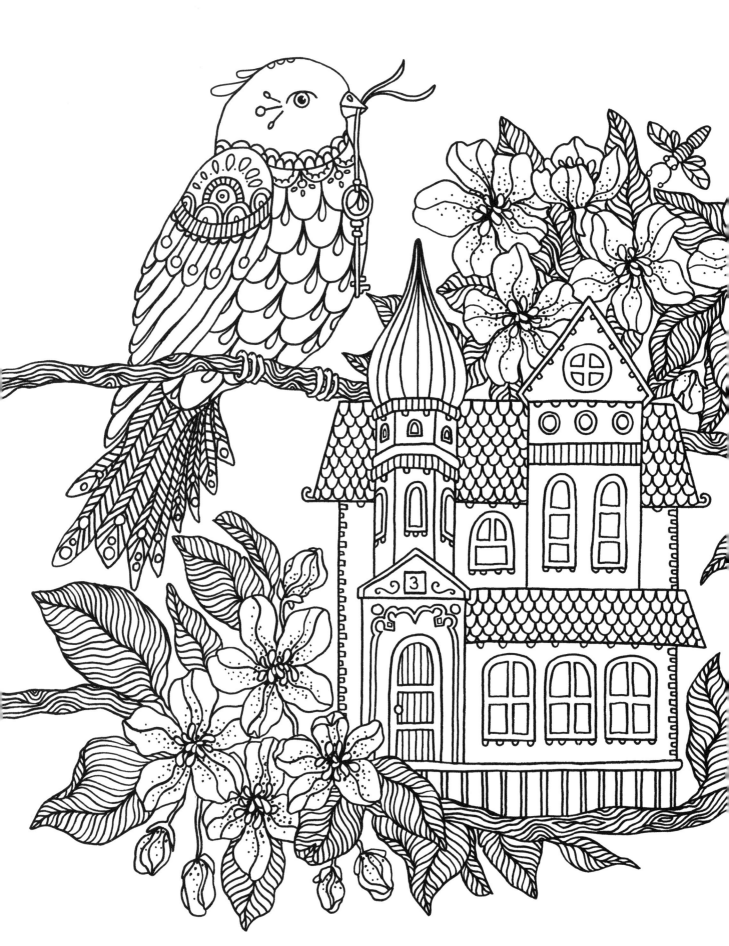

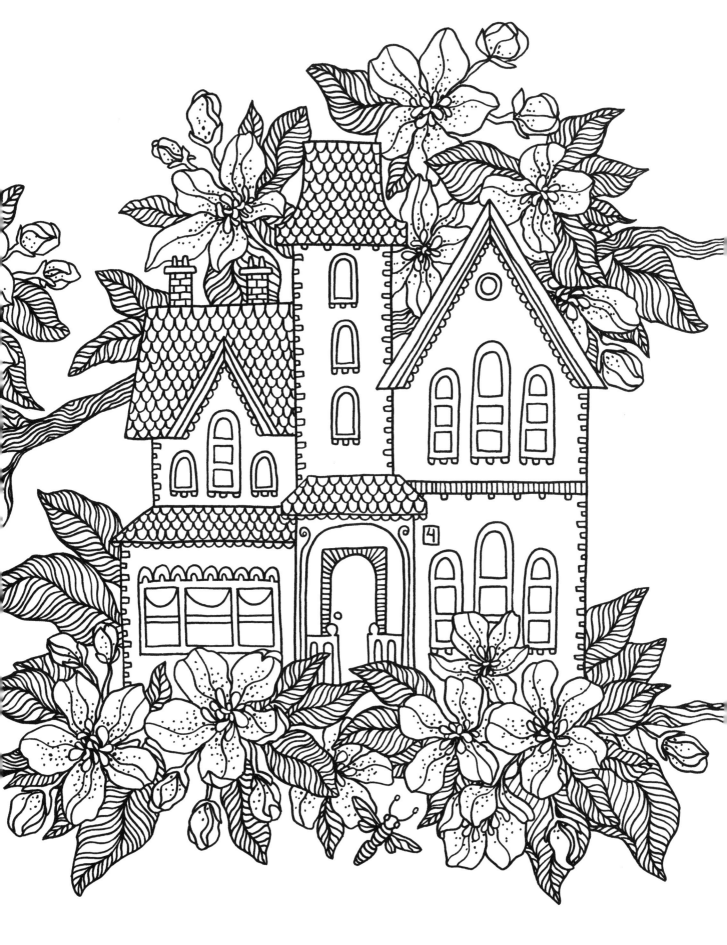

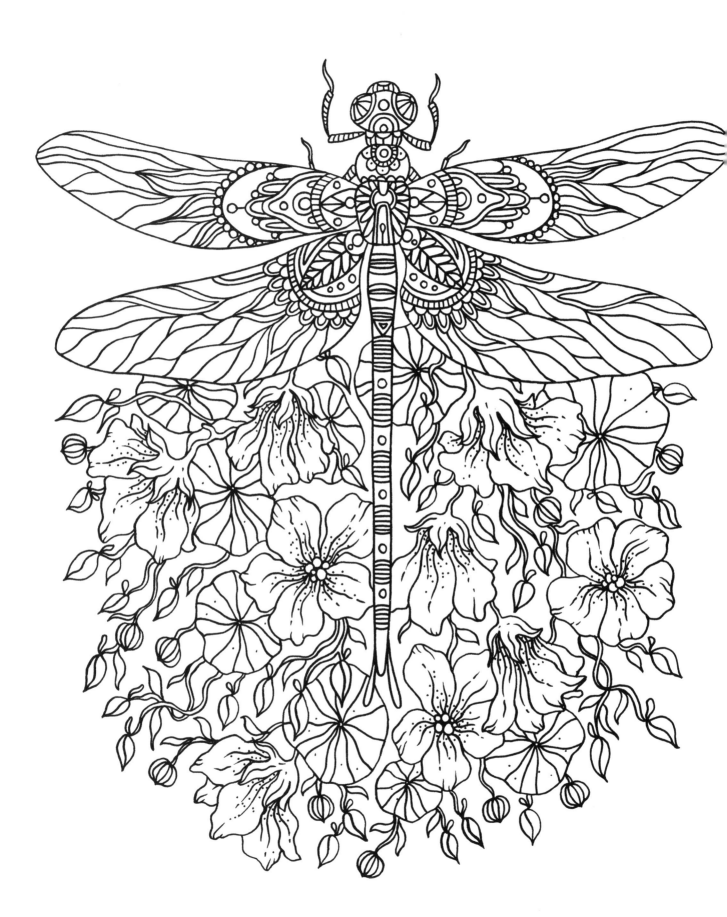

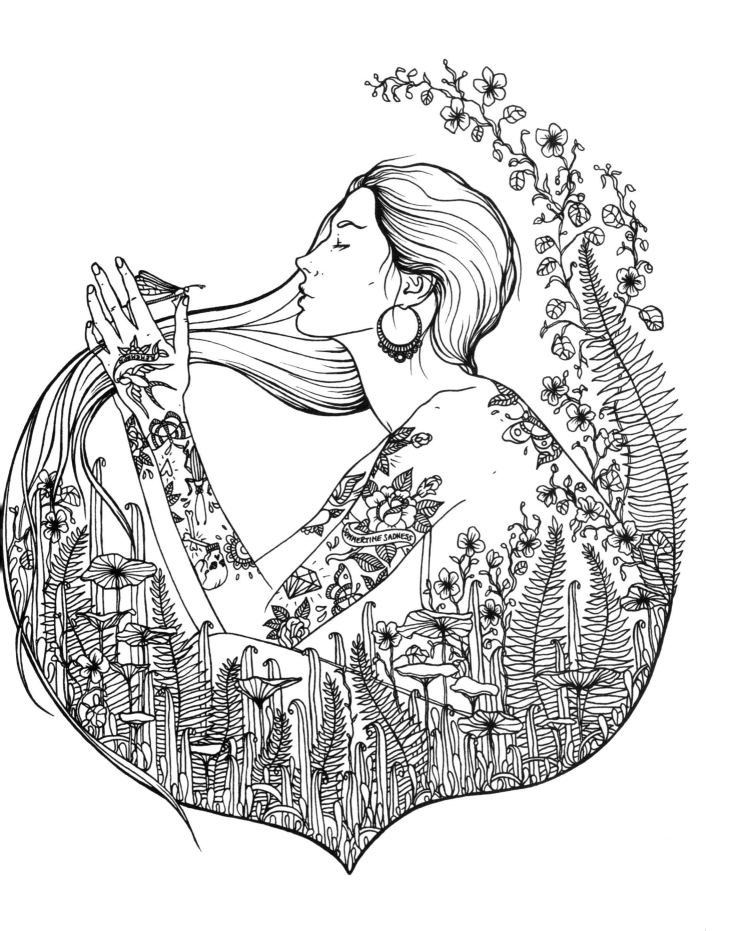

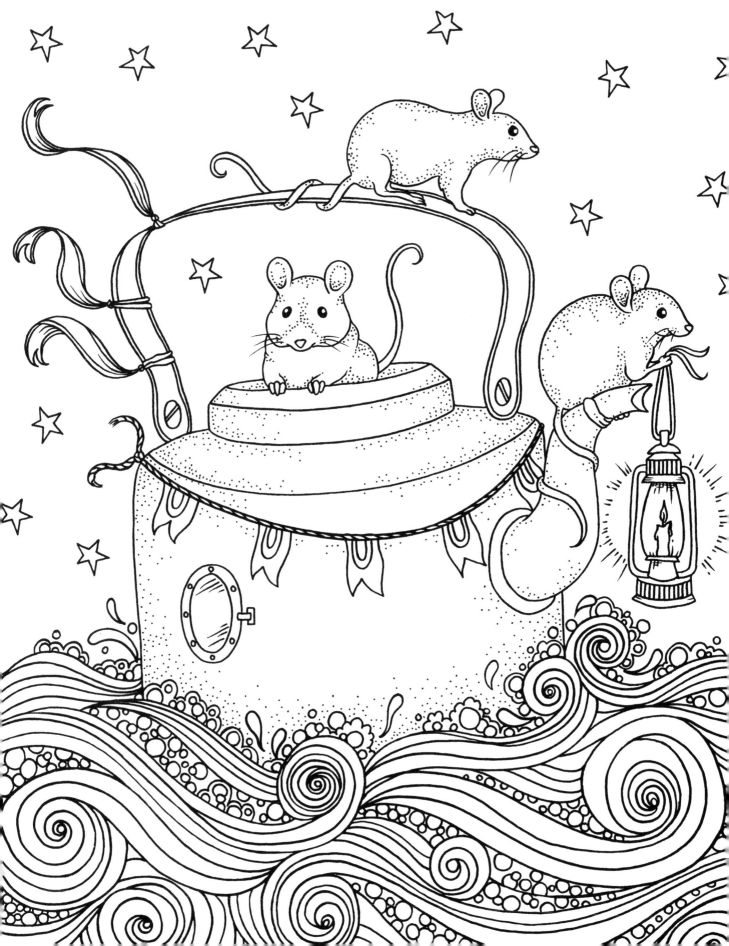

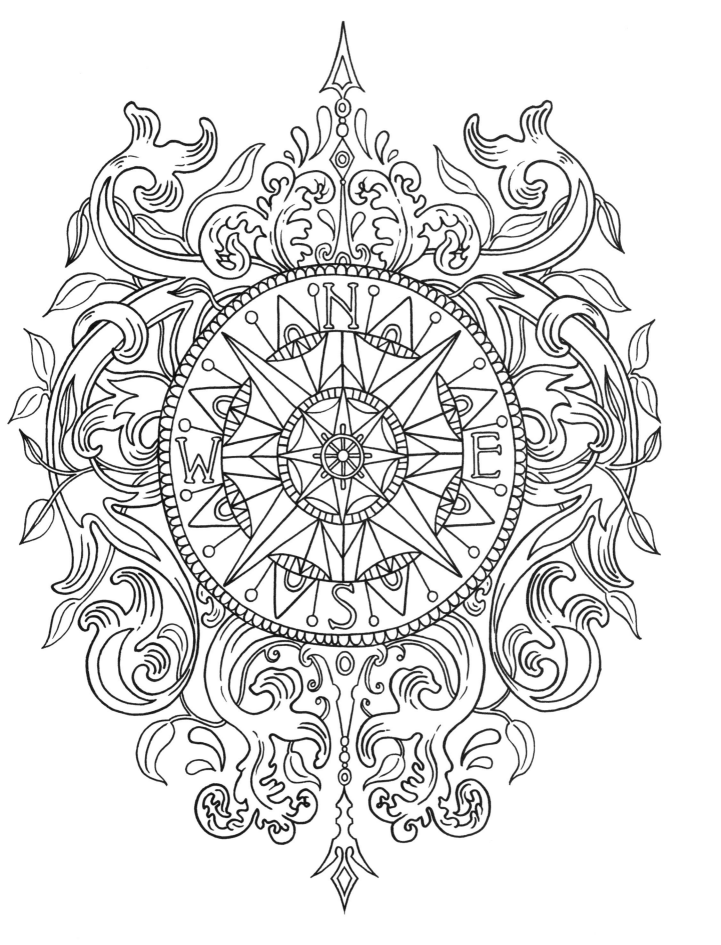

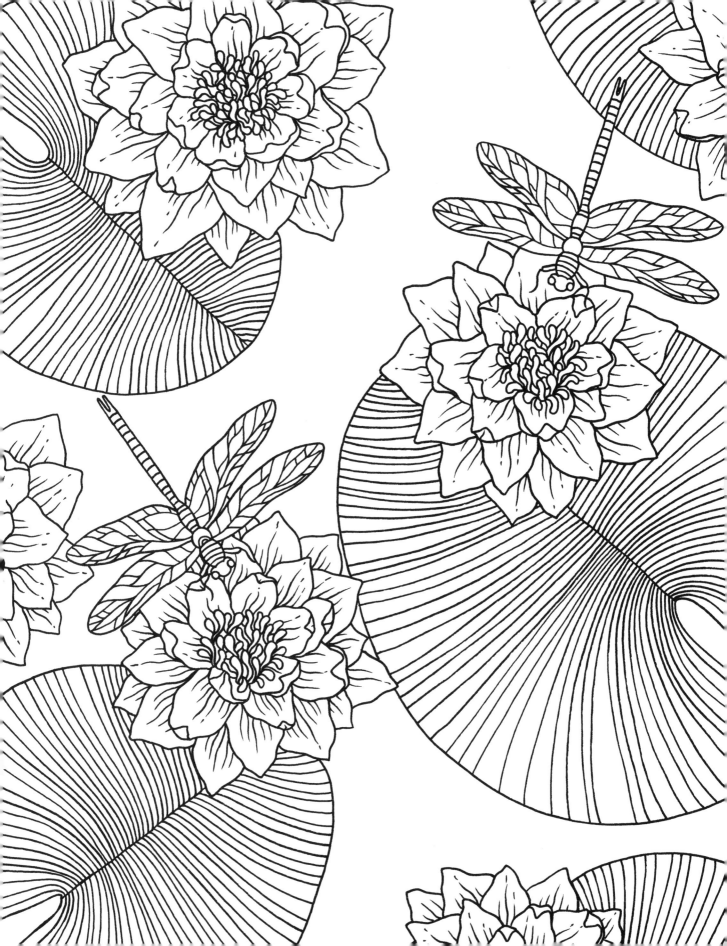

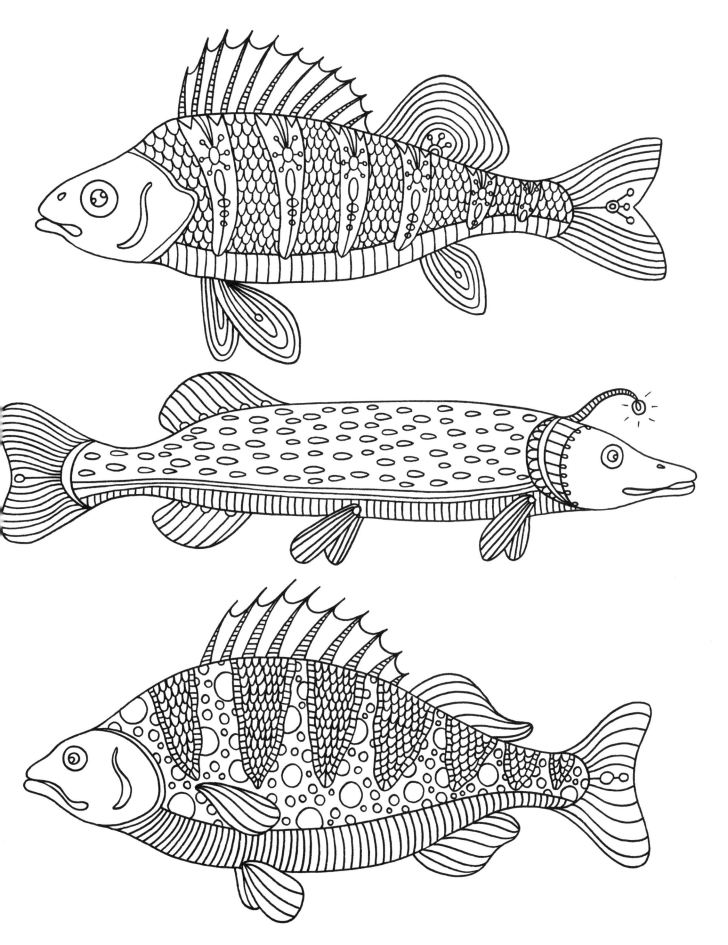

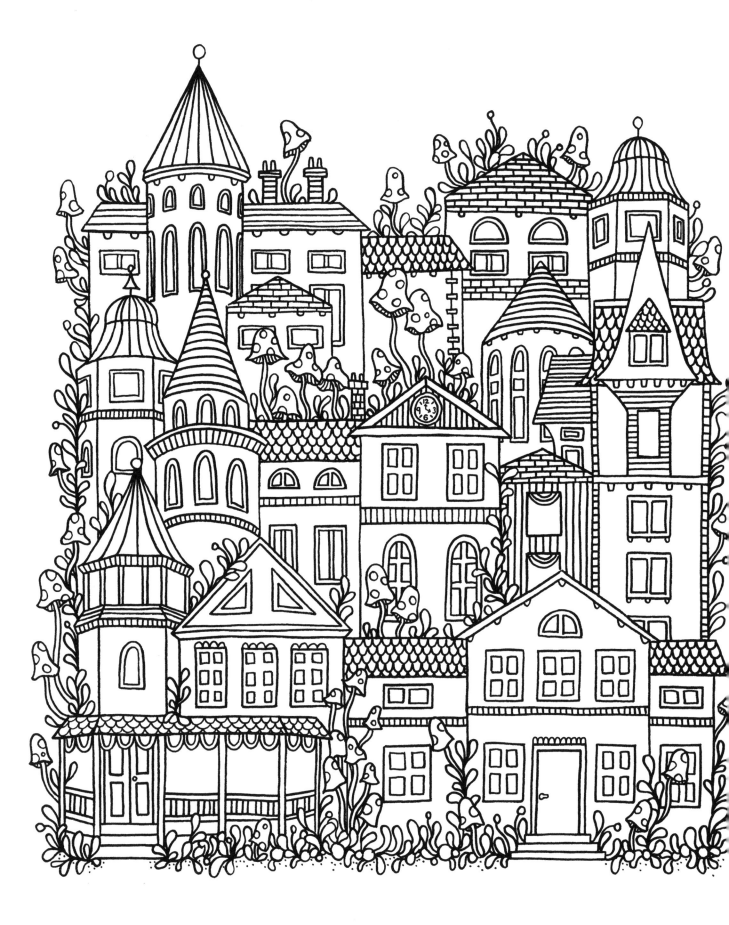

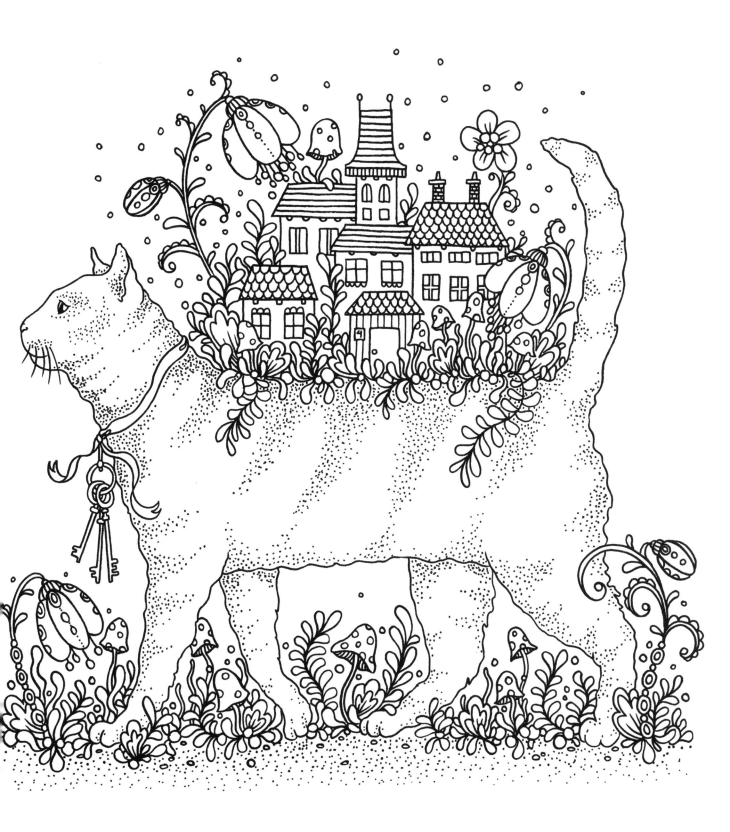

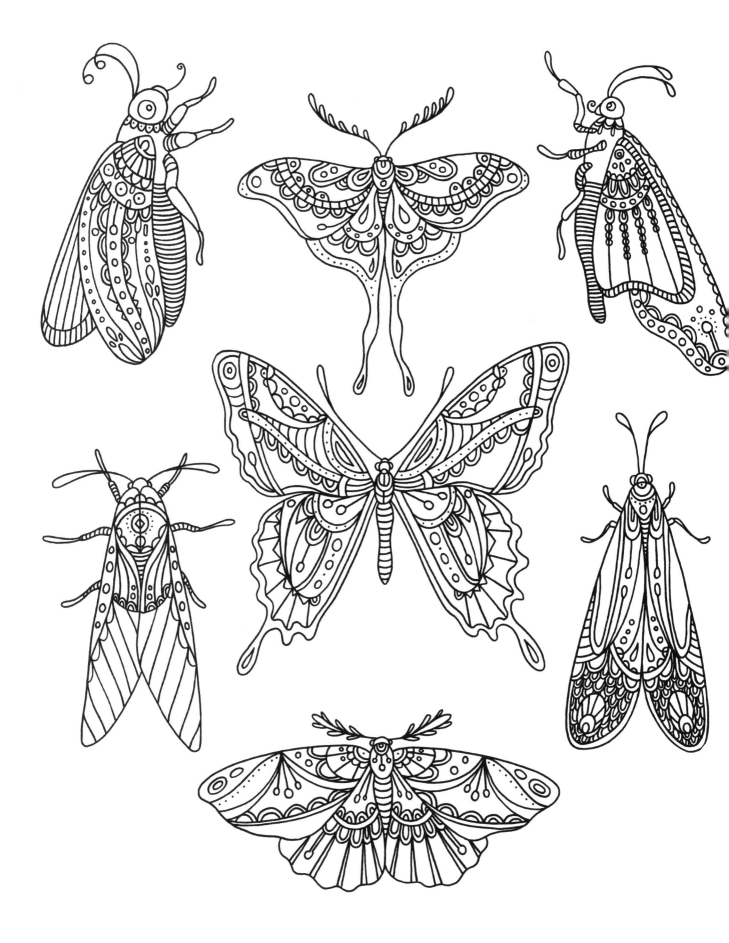

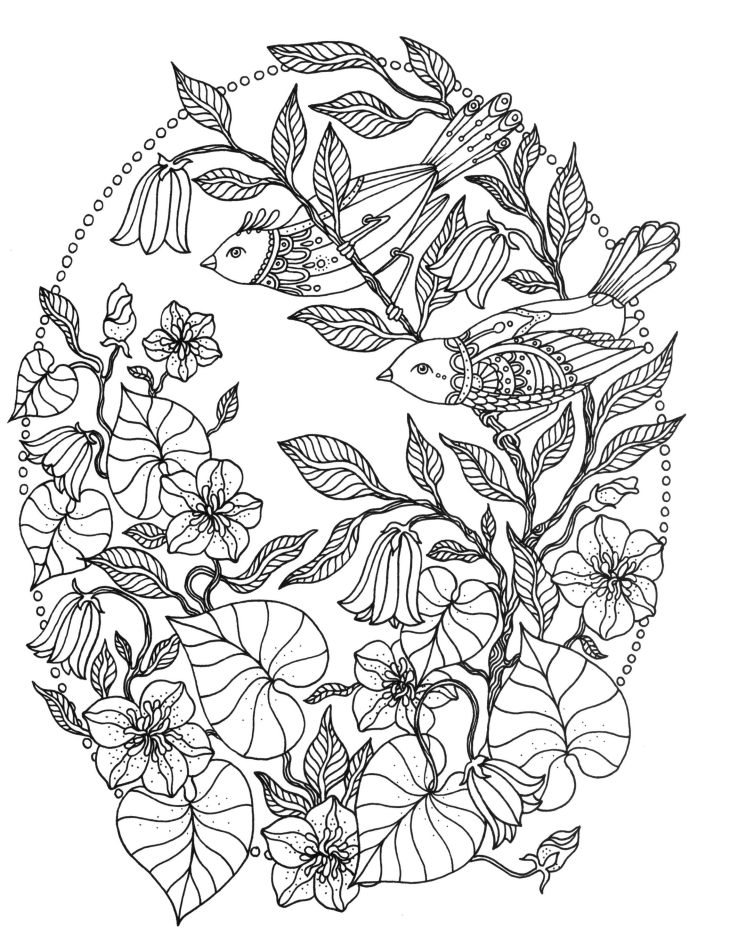

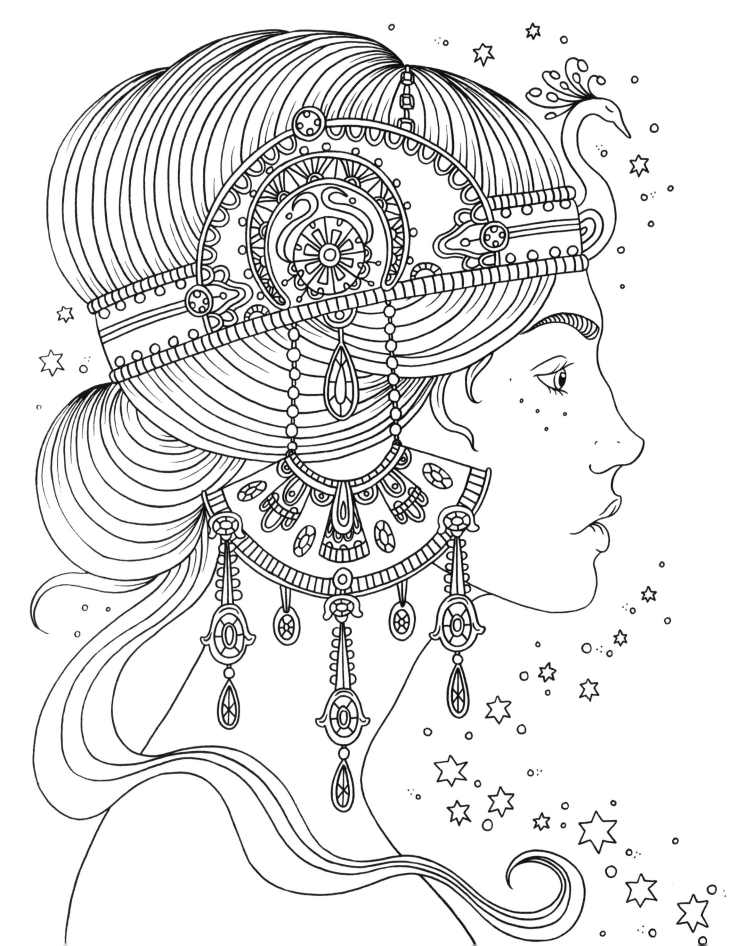

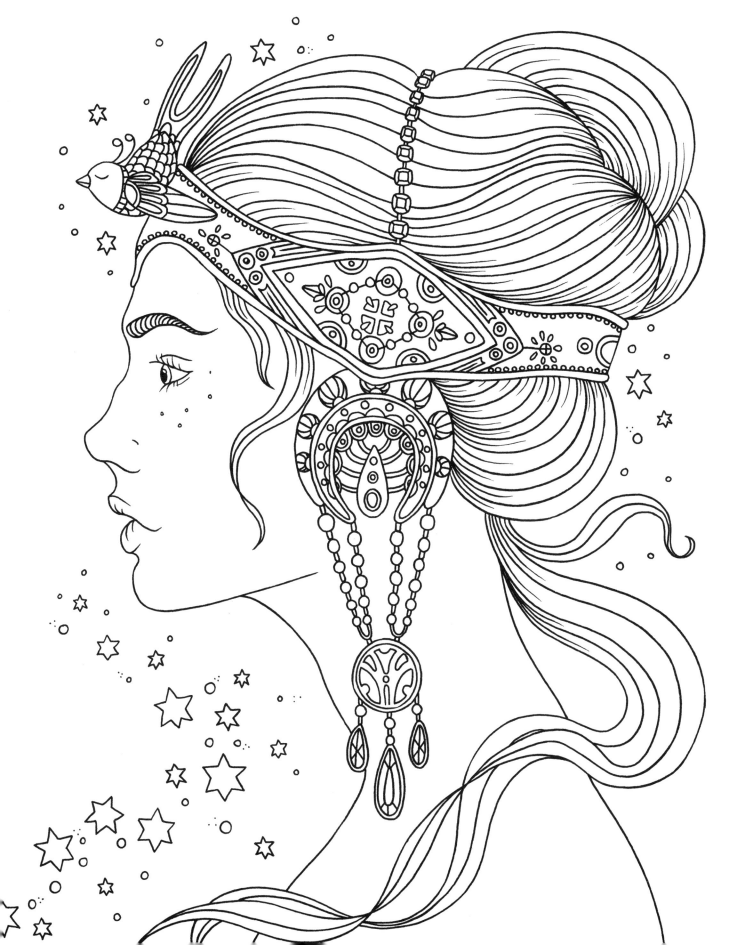

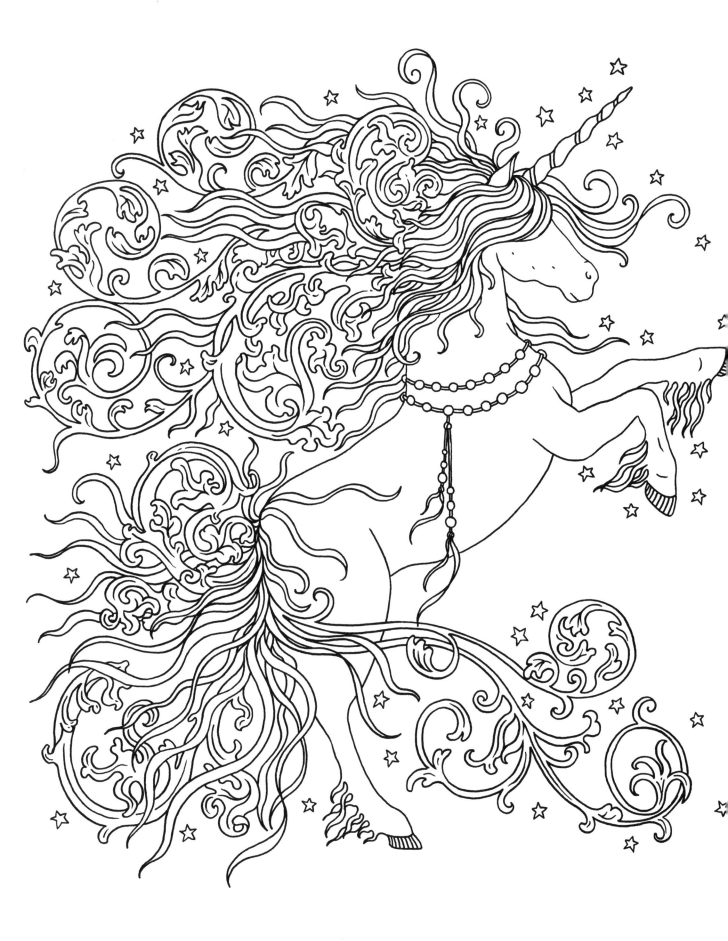

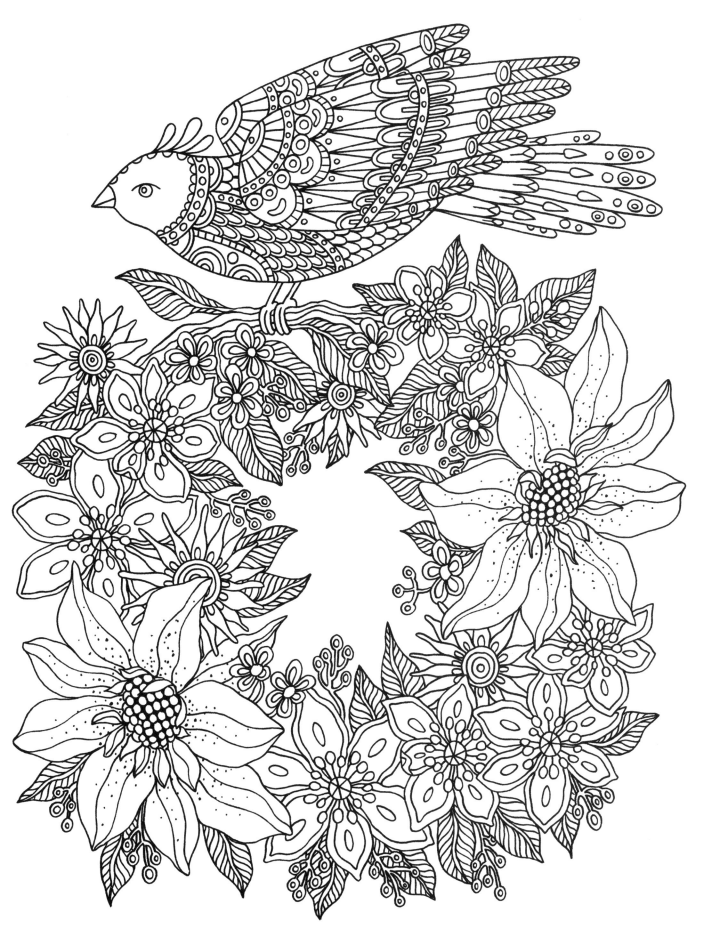

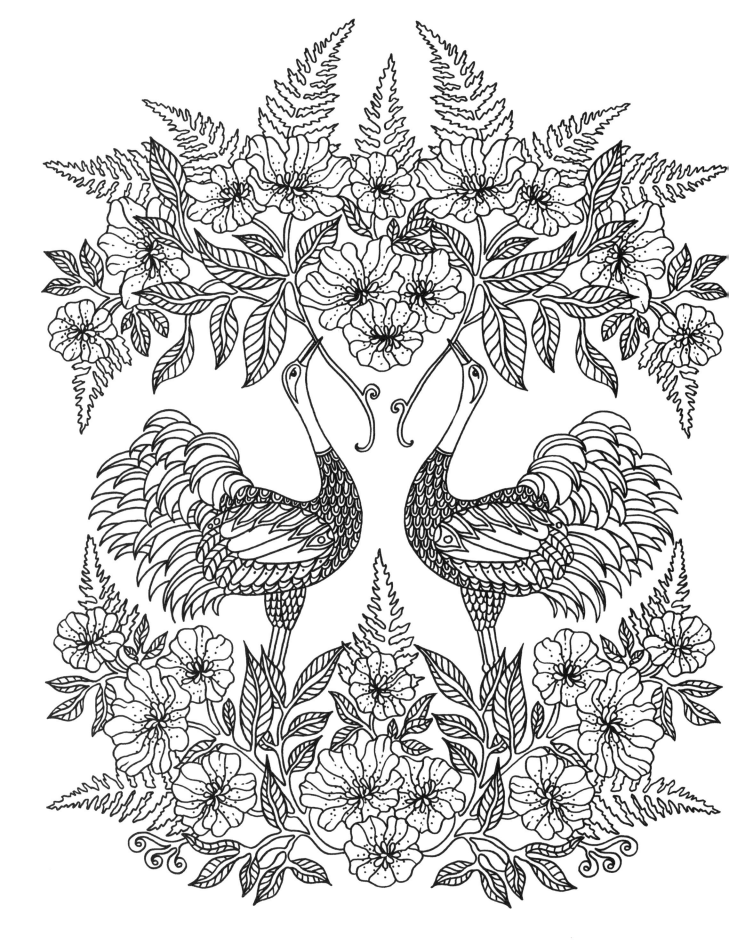

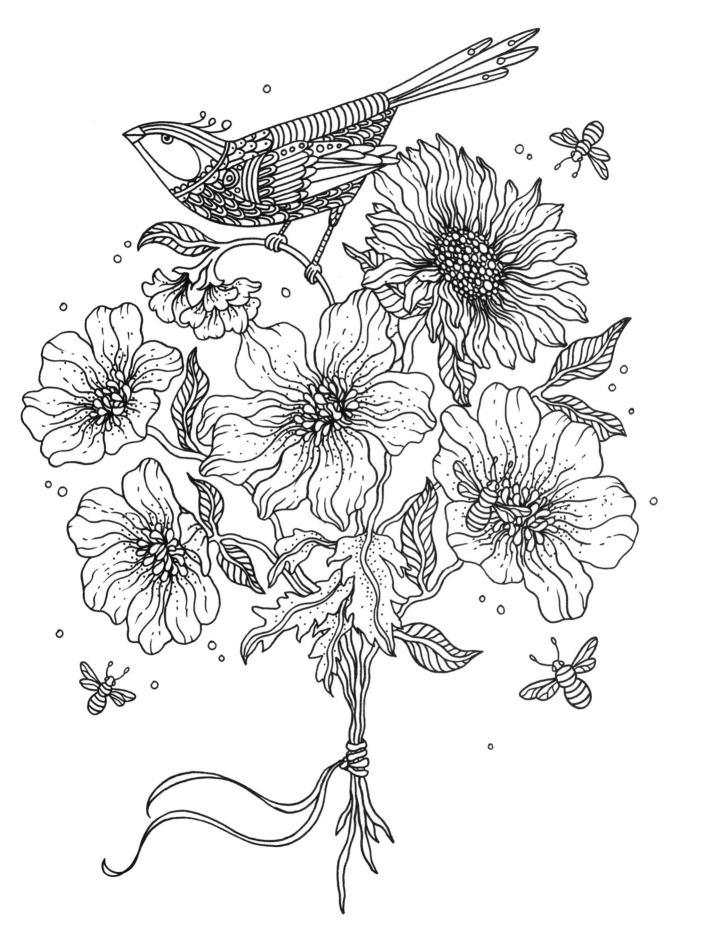

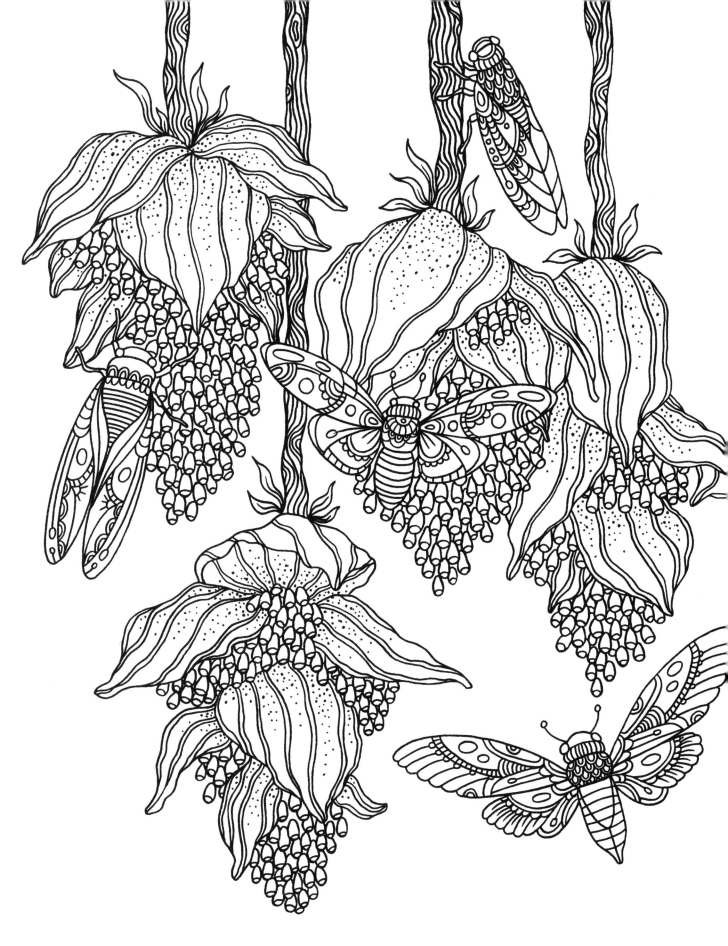

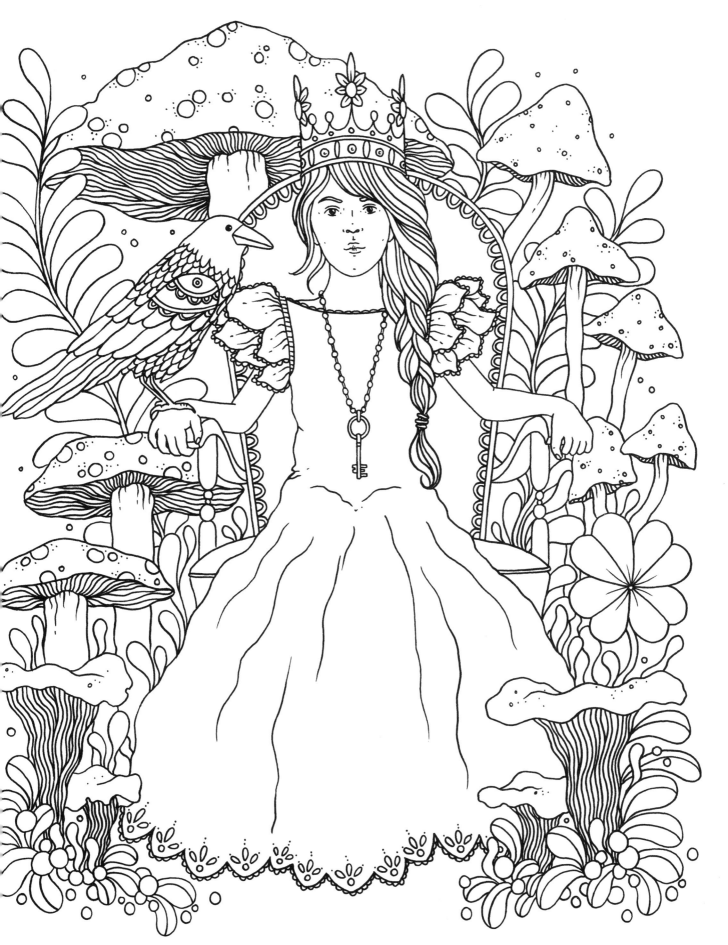

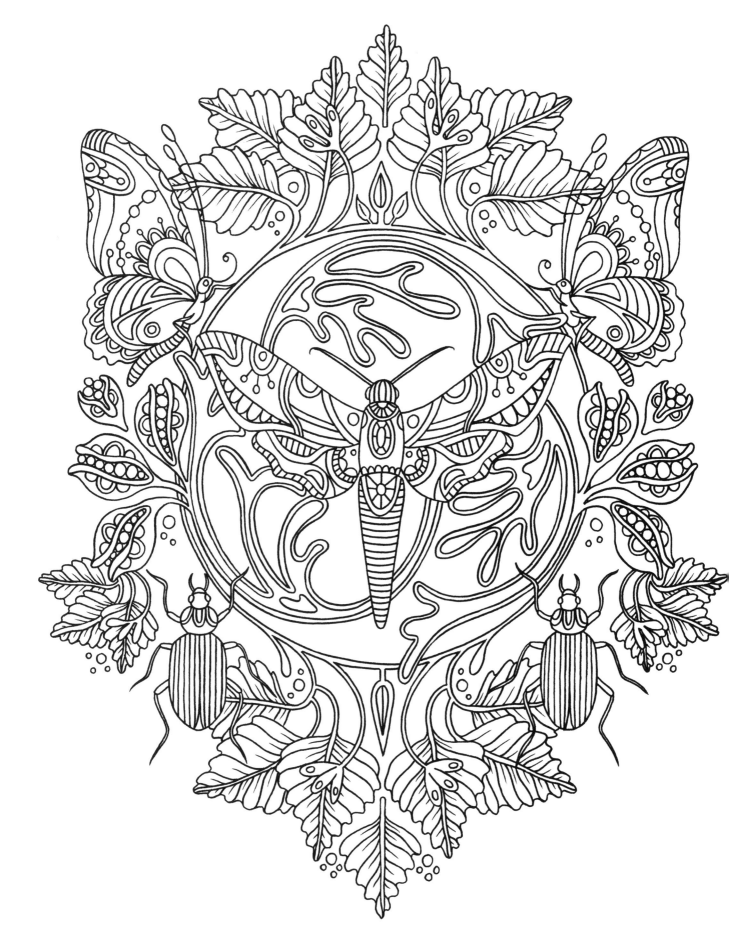

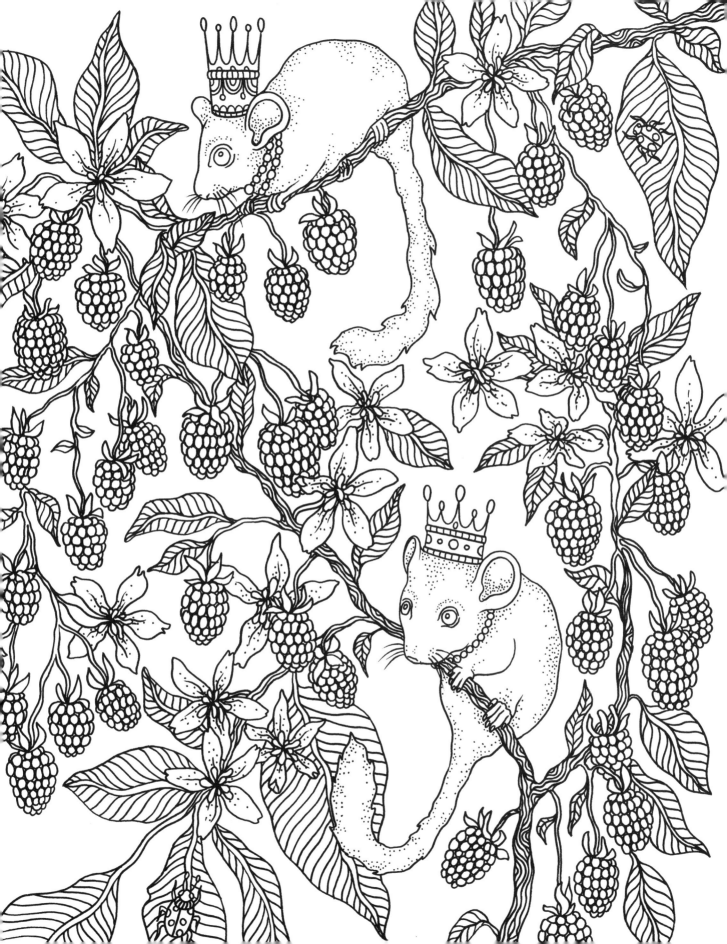

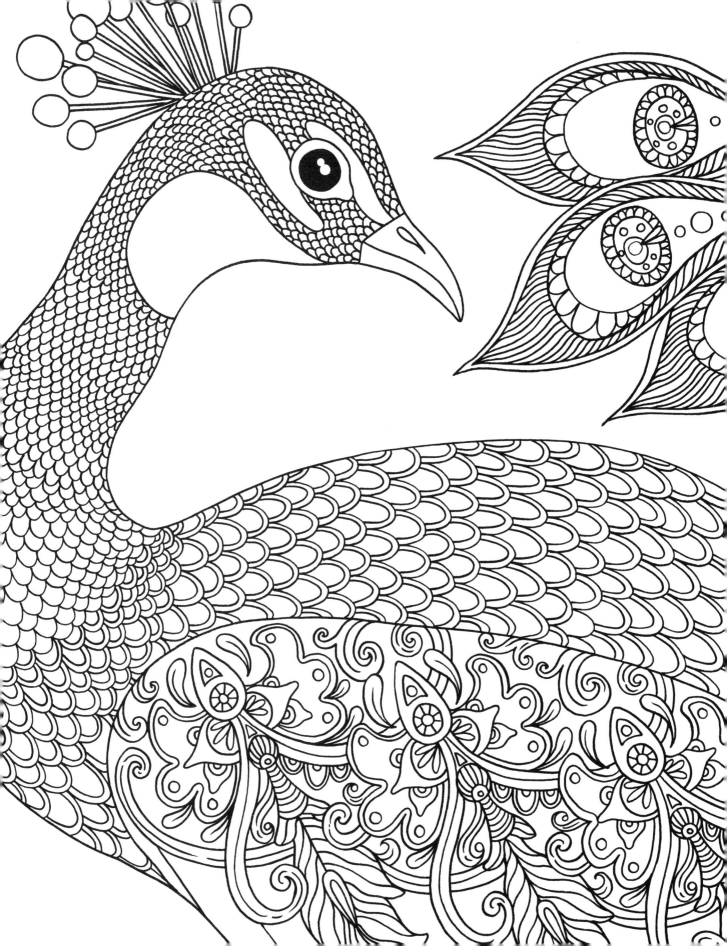

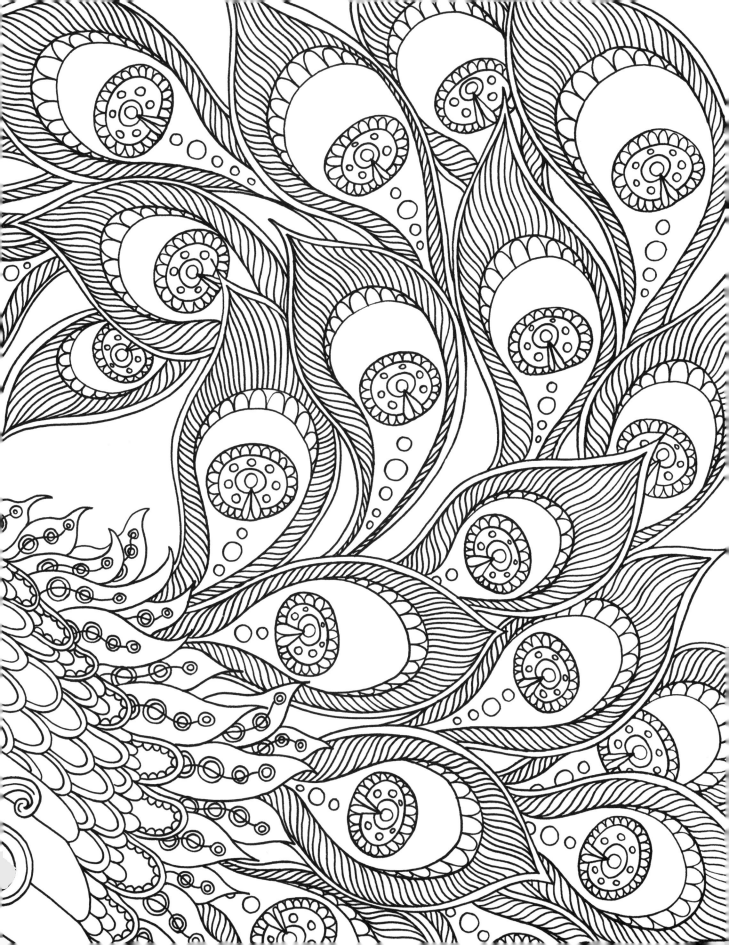

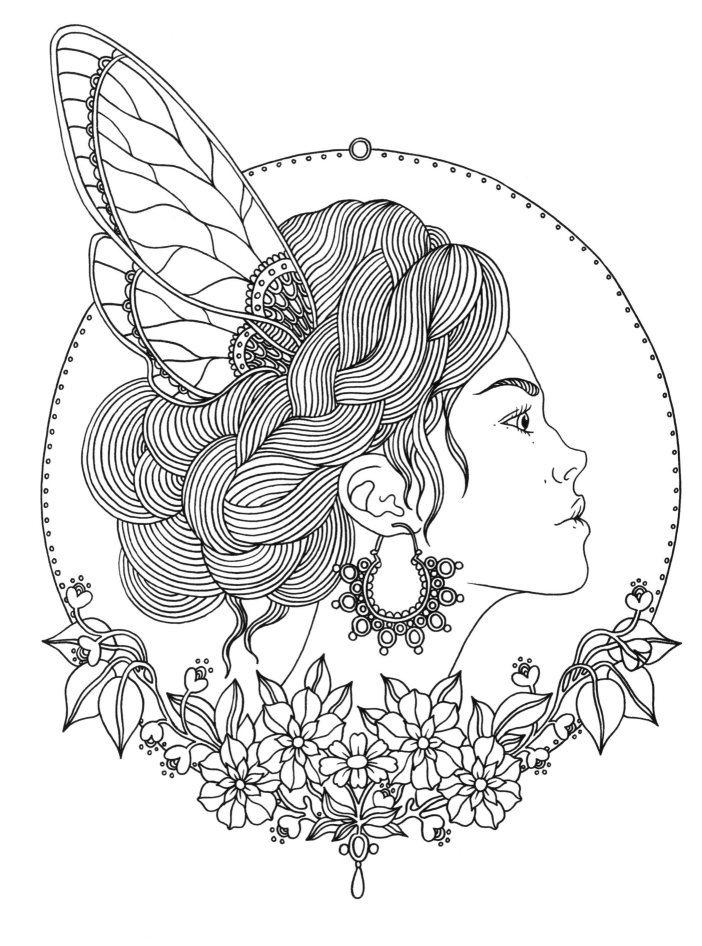

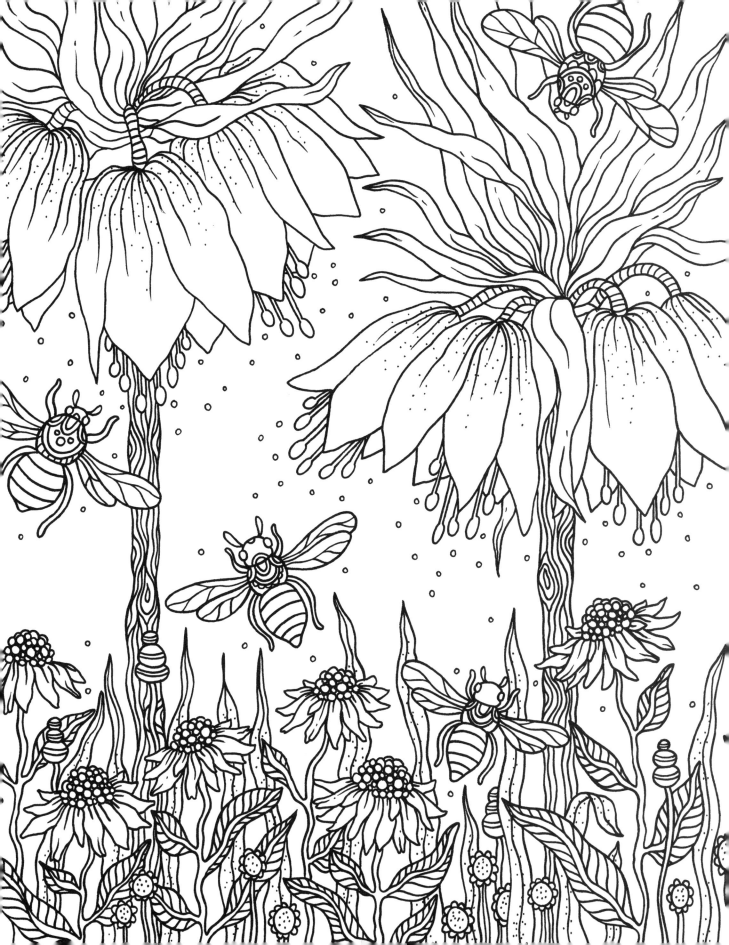

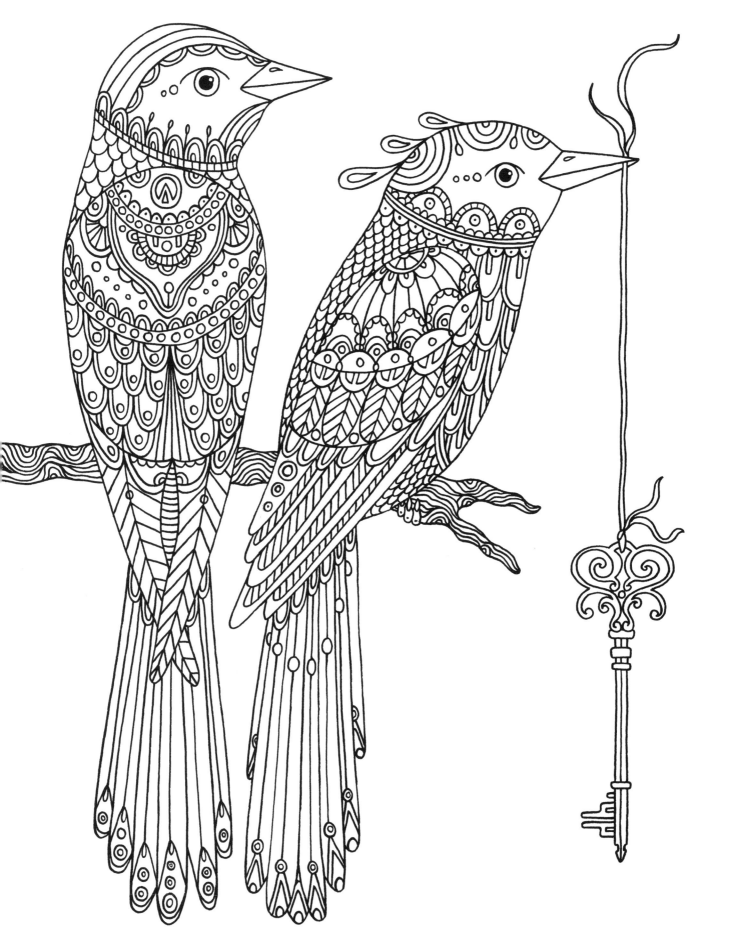

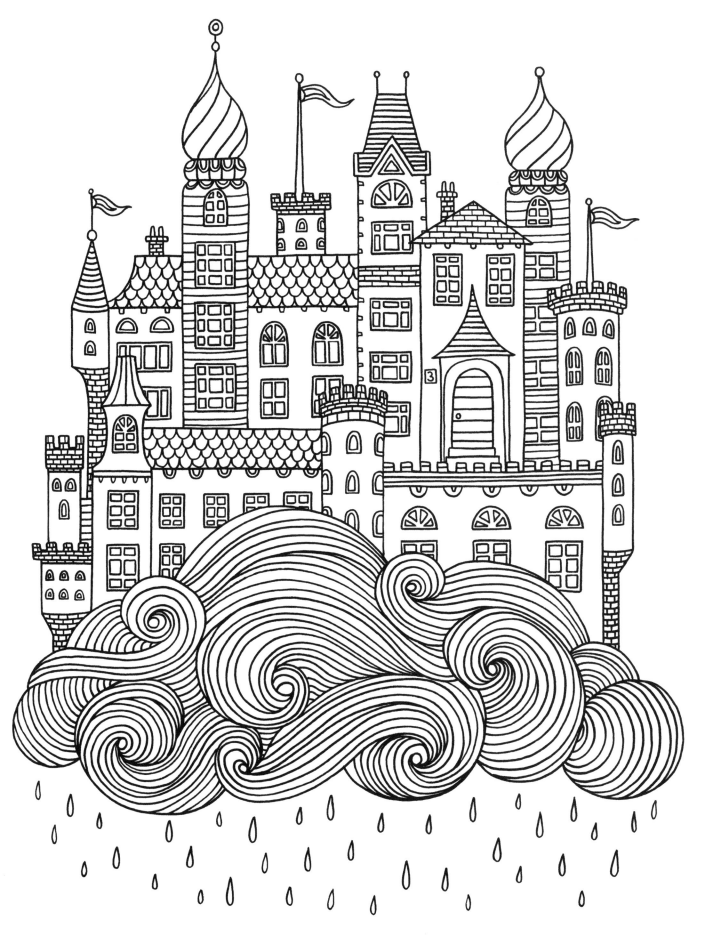

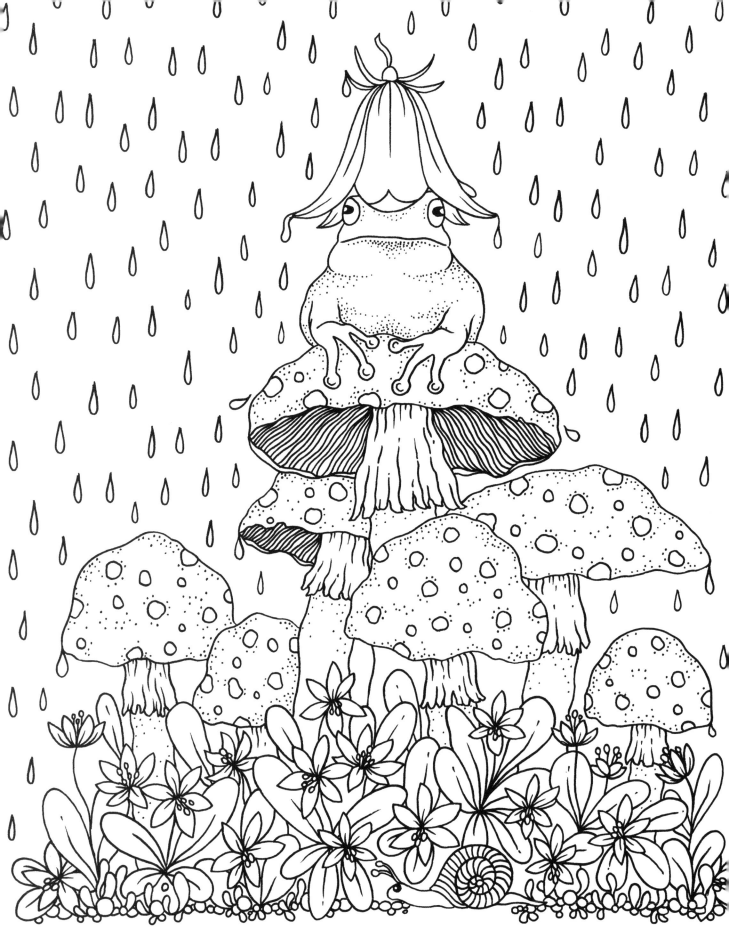

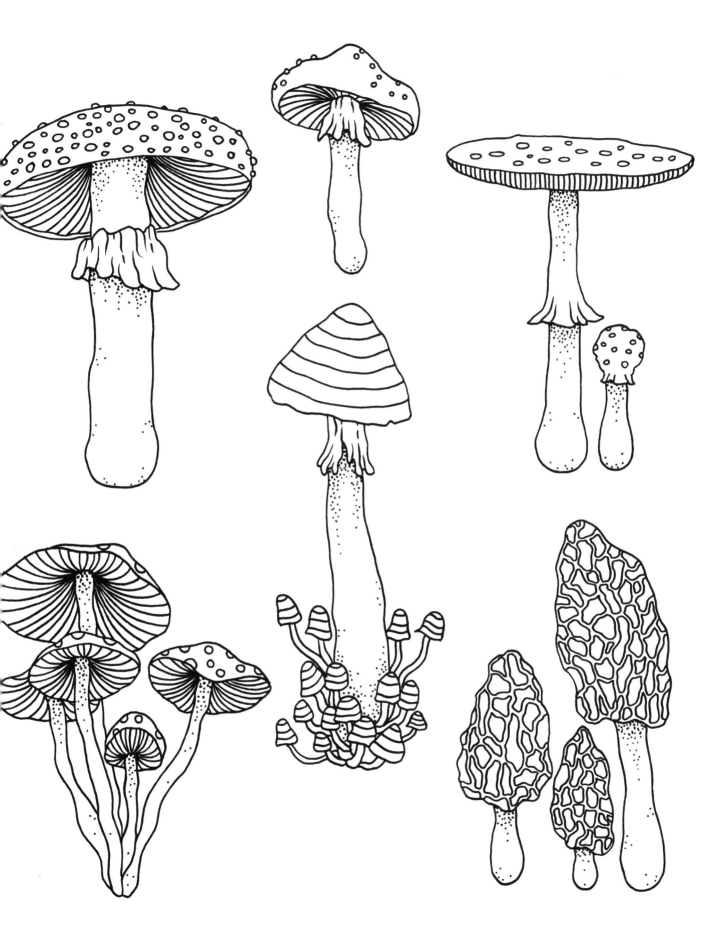

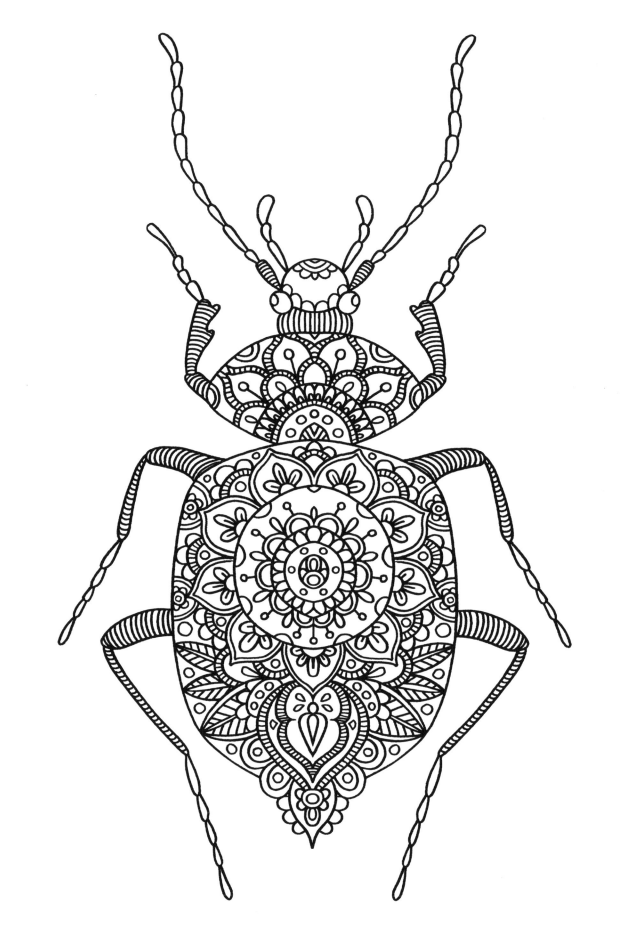

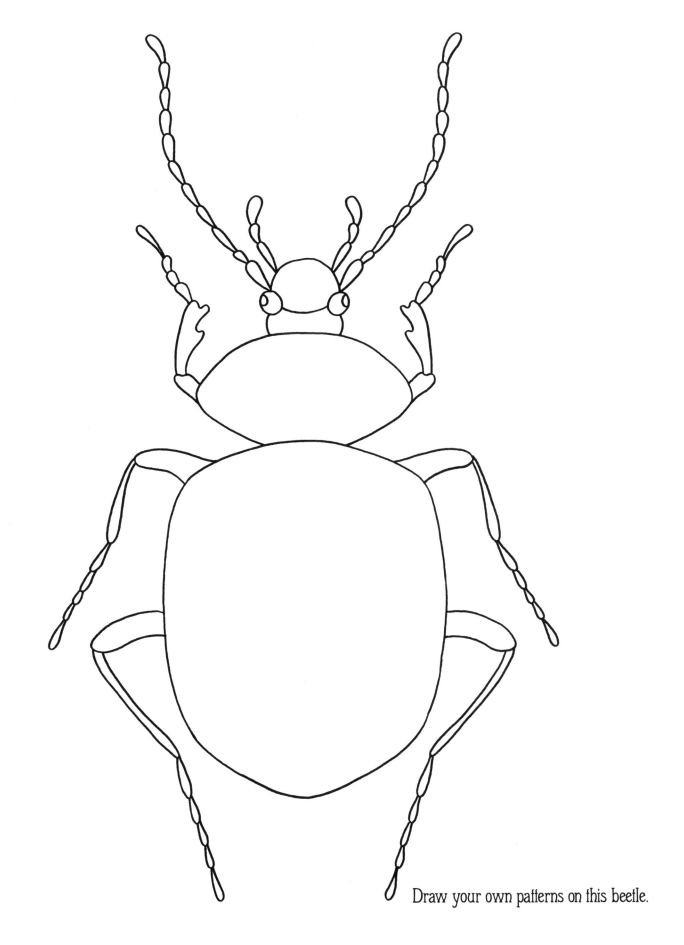

Draw your own patterns on this beetle.

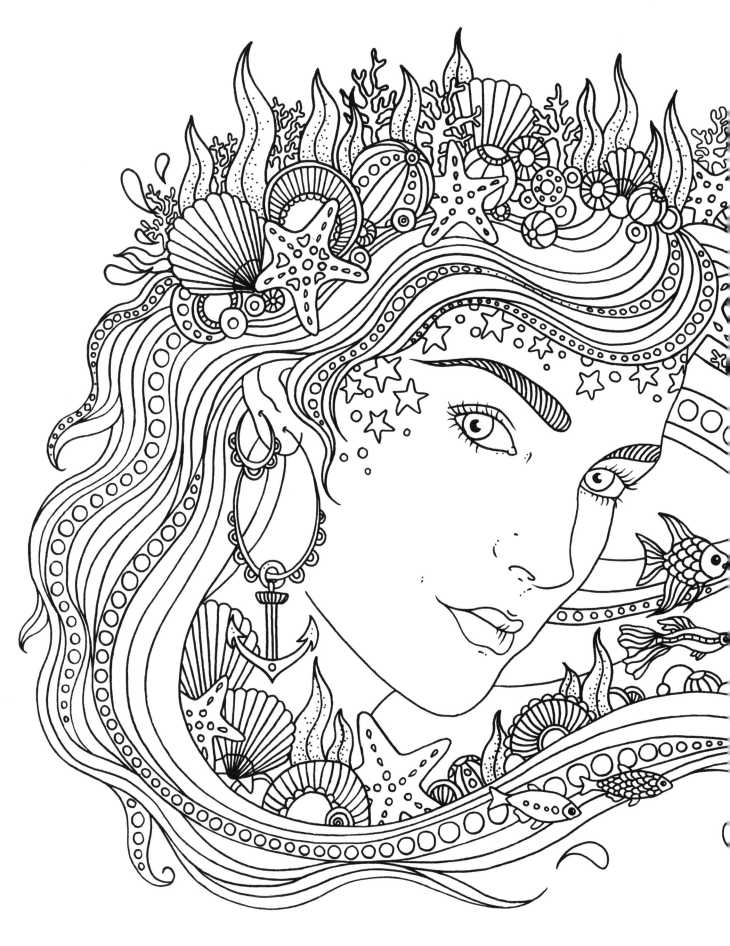

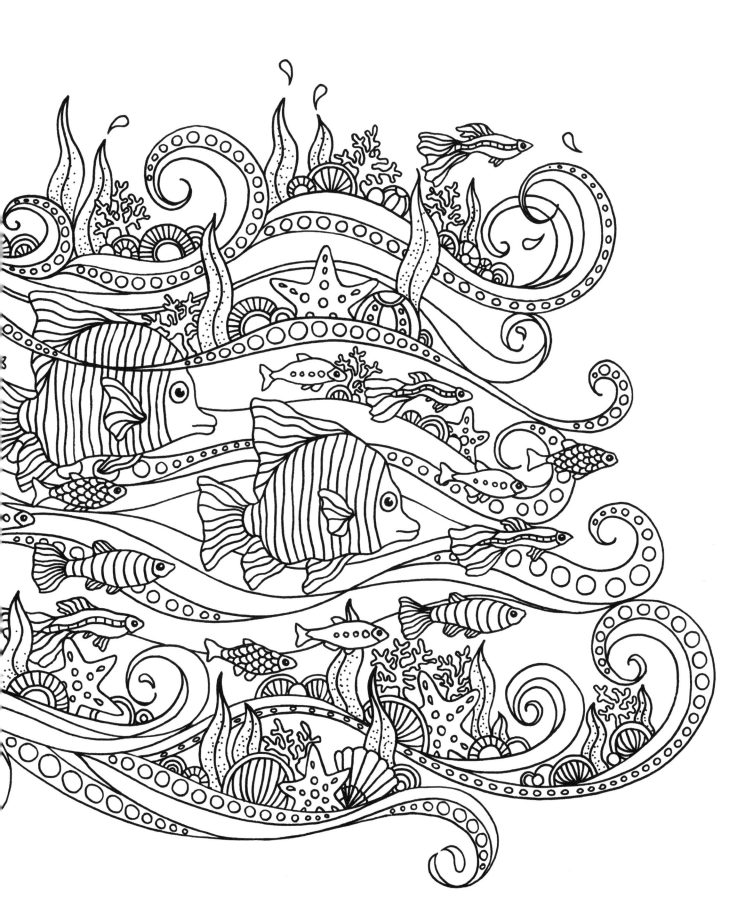

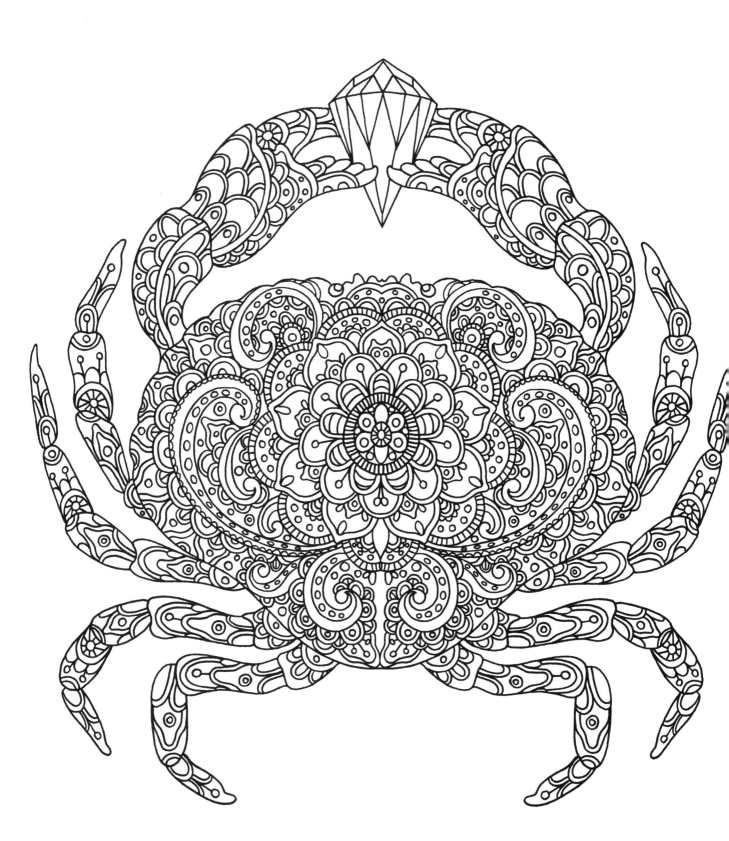

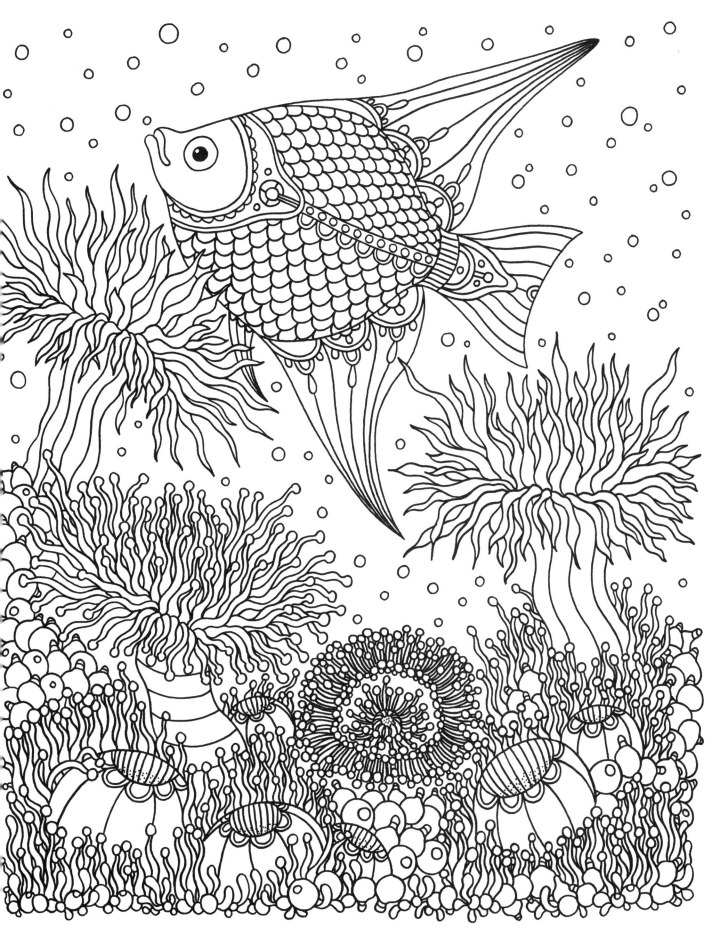

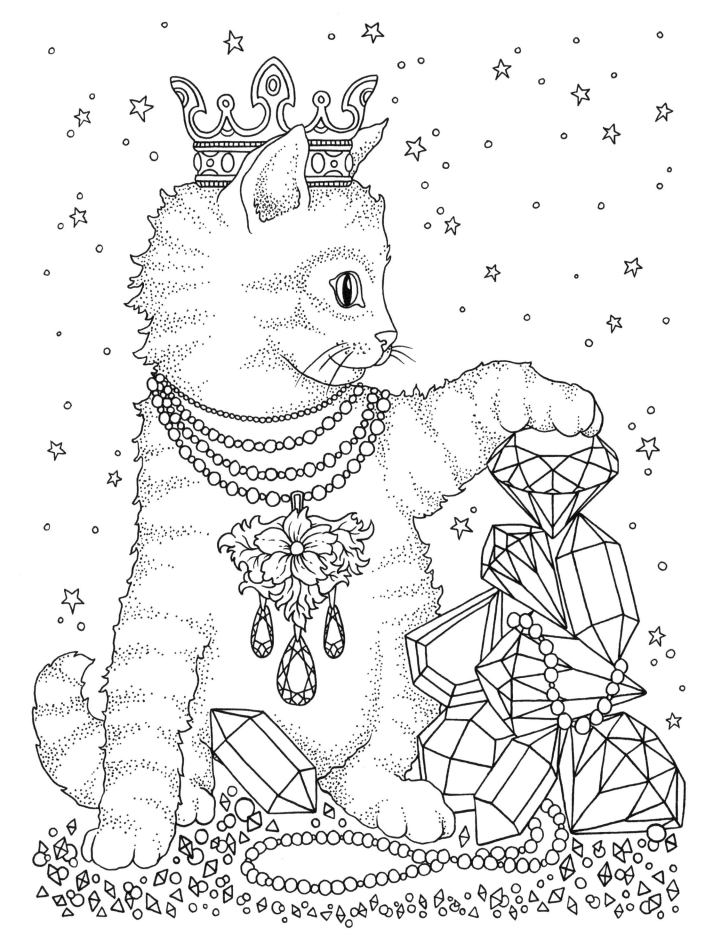

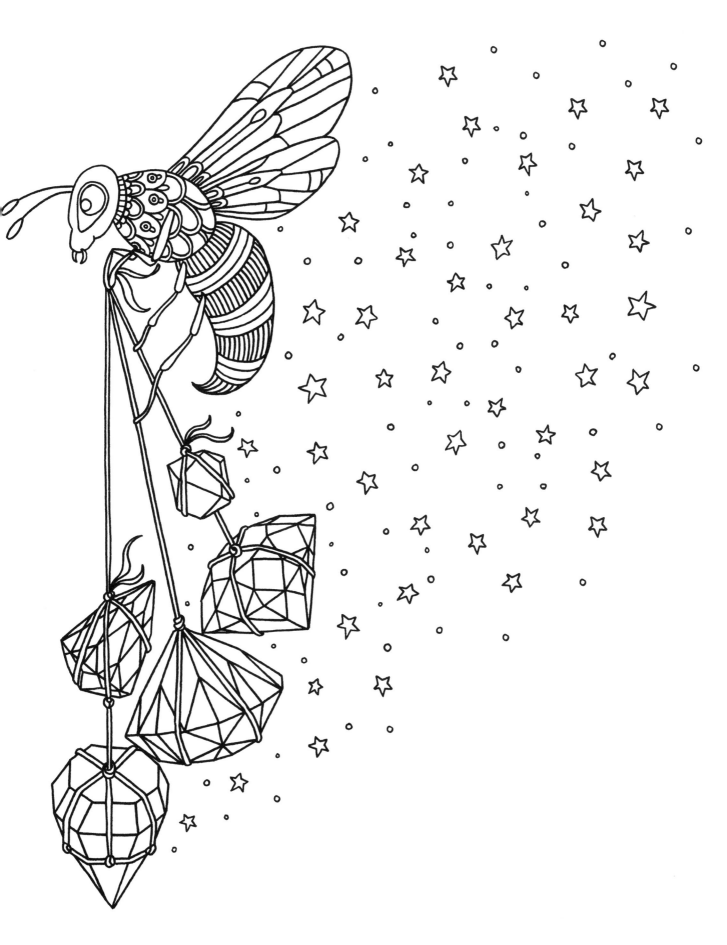

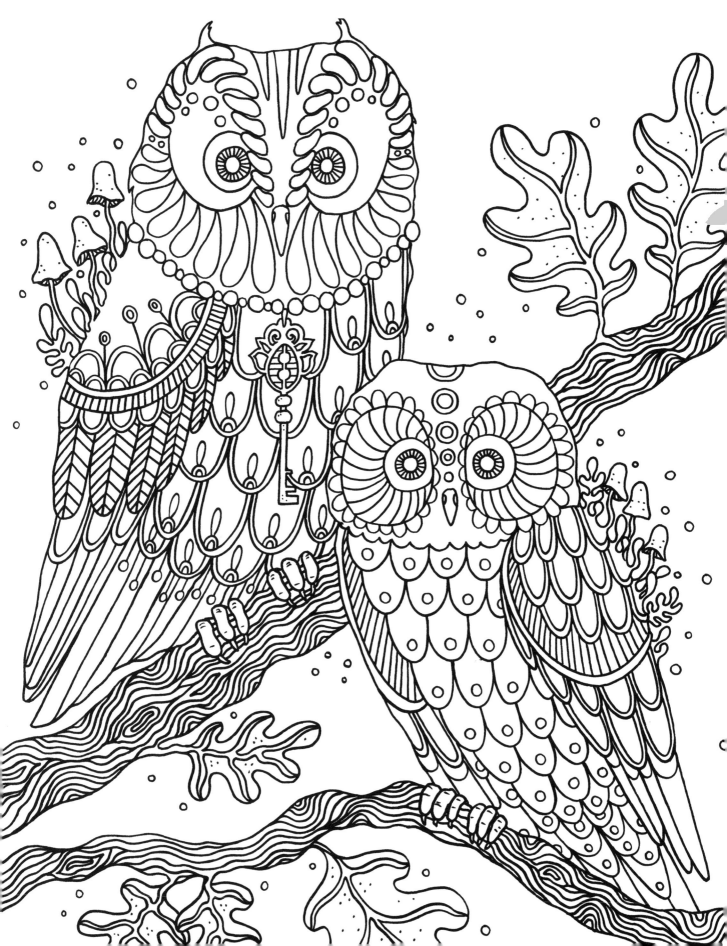

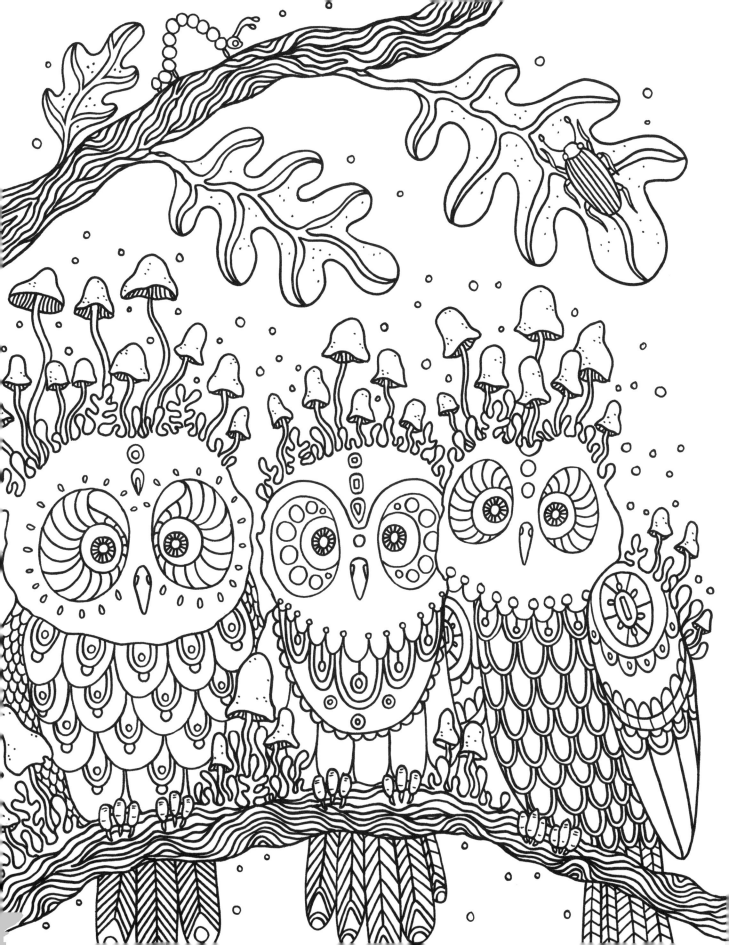

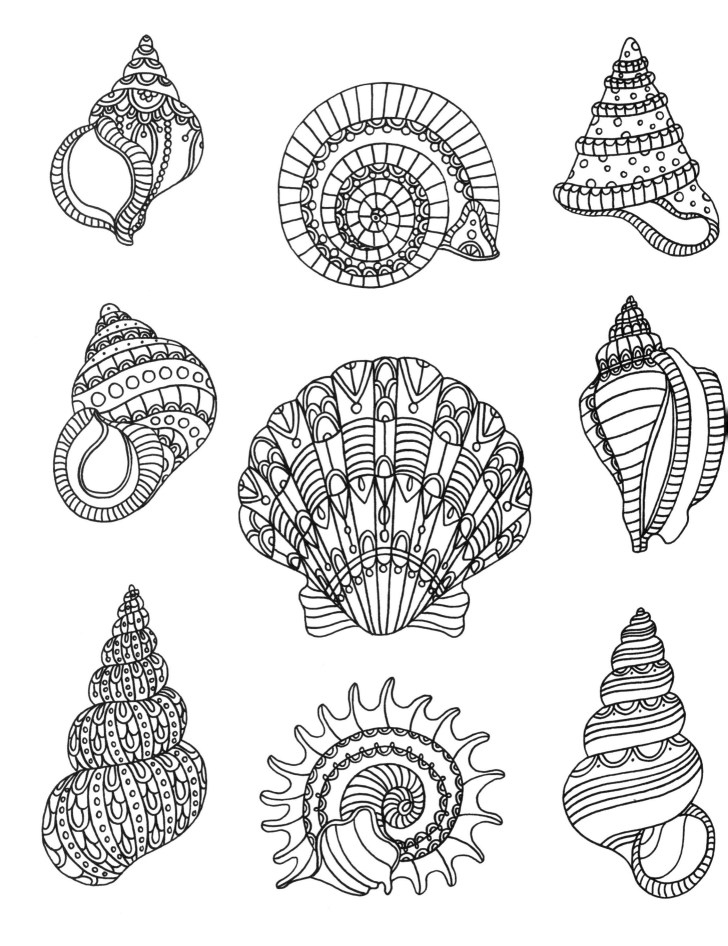

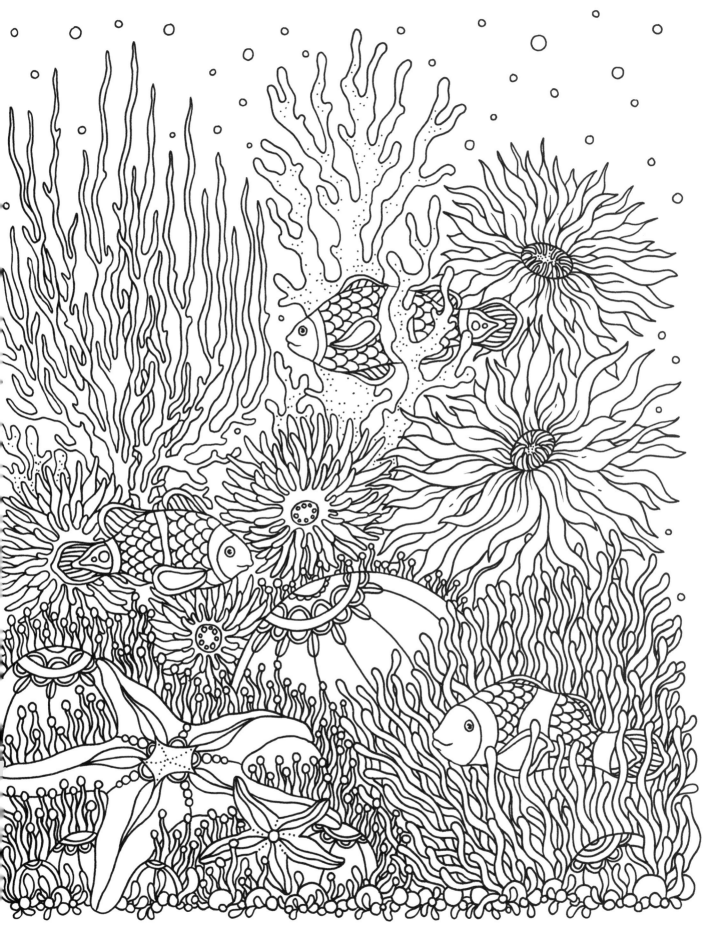

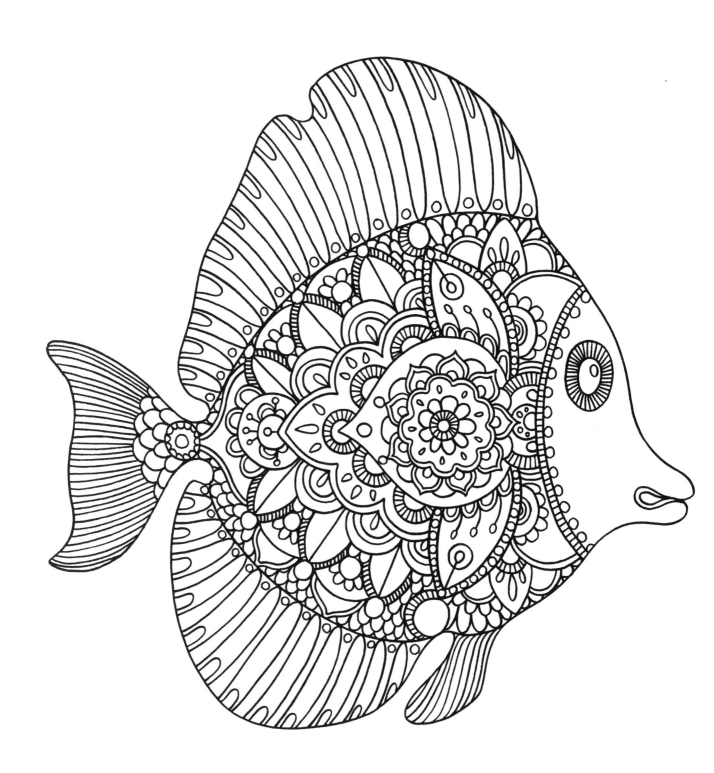

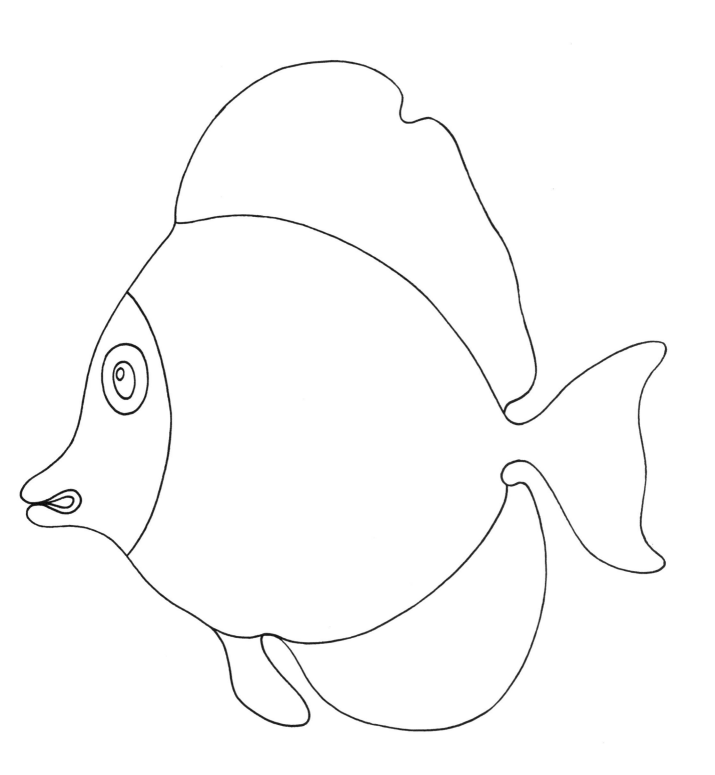

Draw your own patterns on this fish.

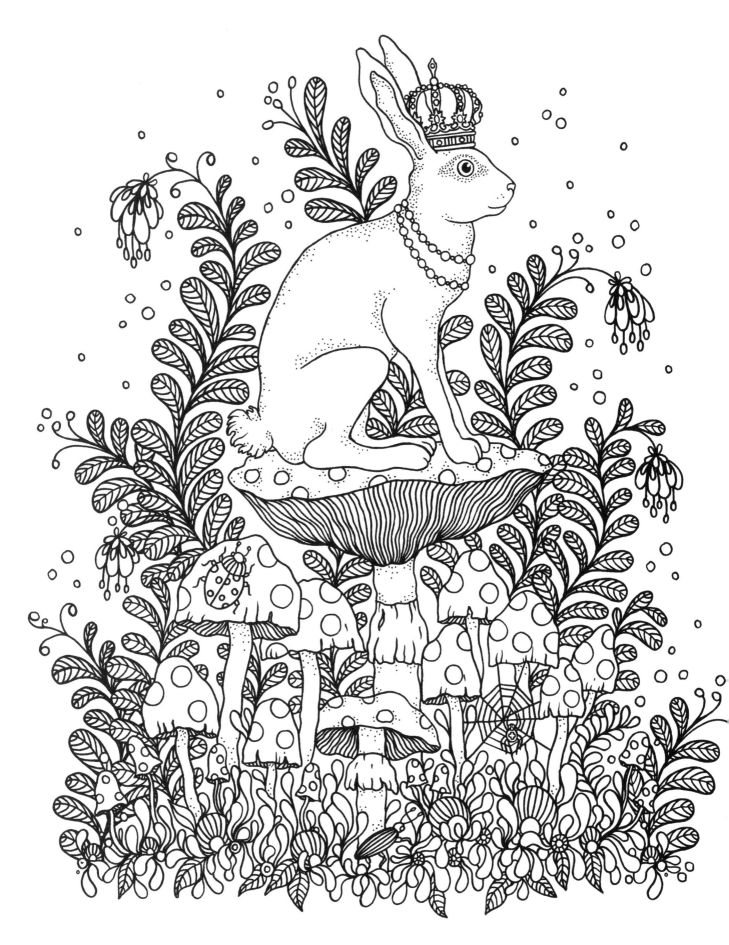

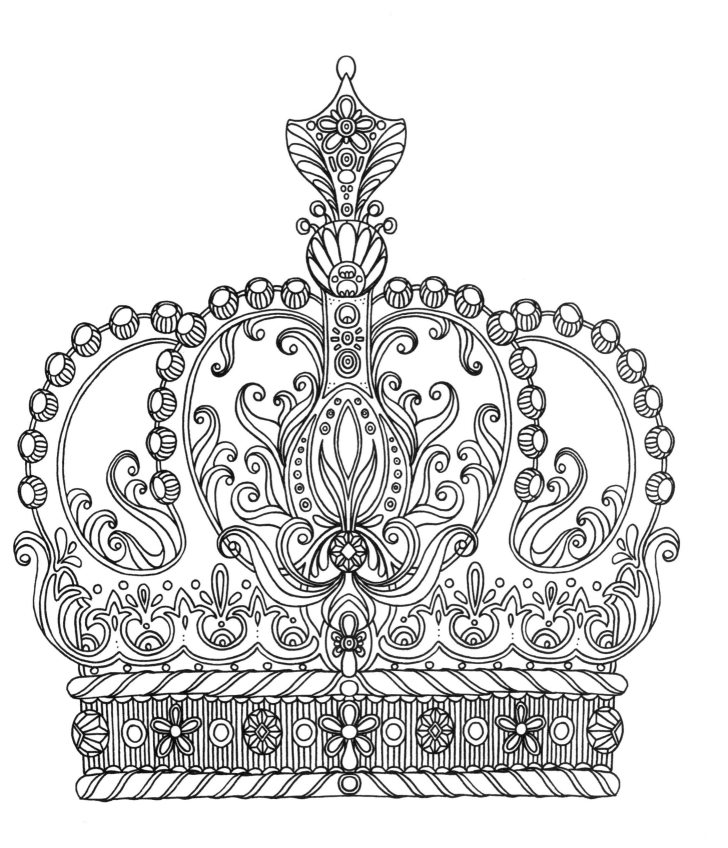

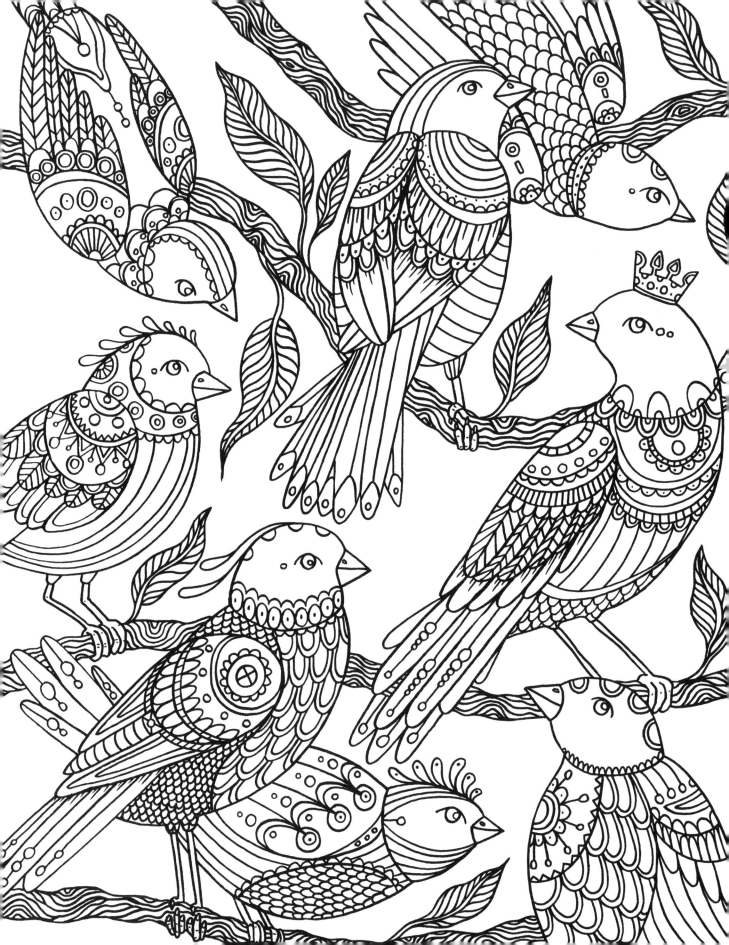

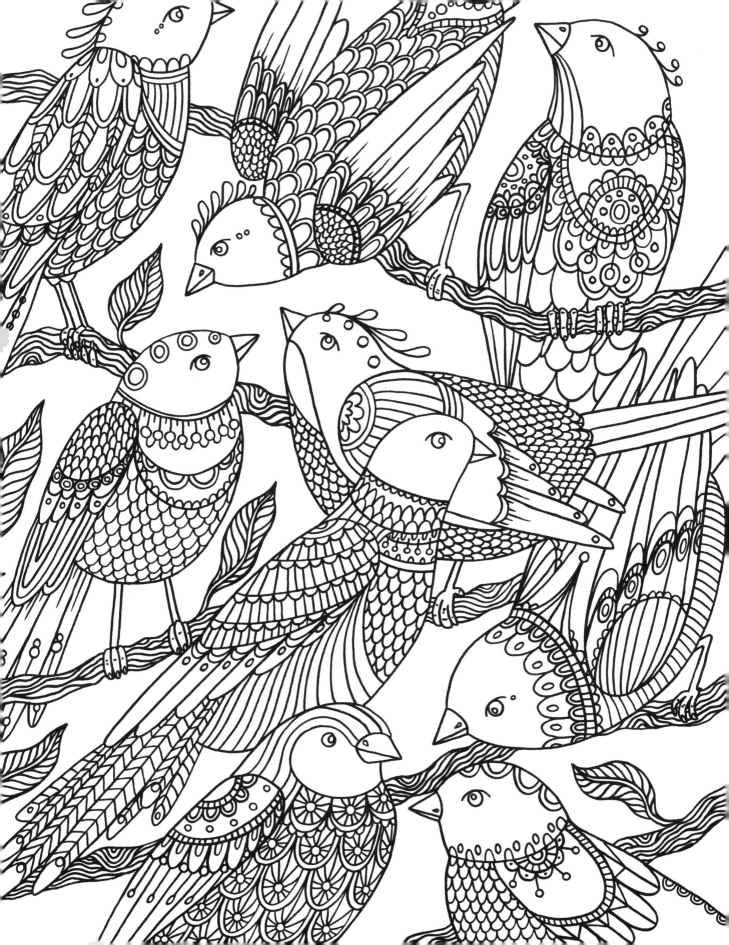

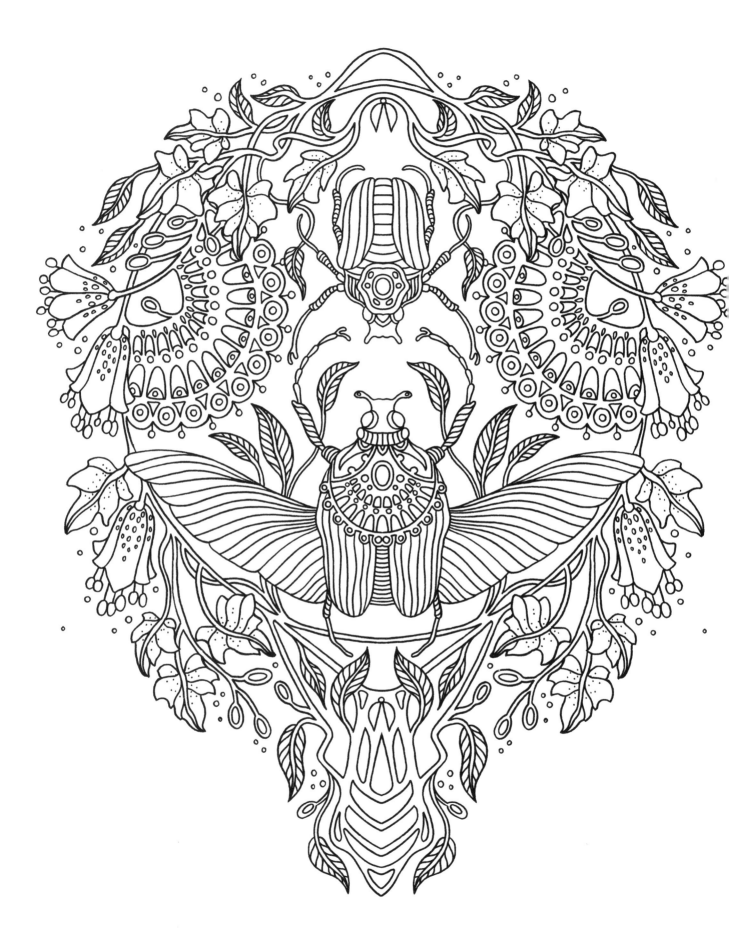

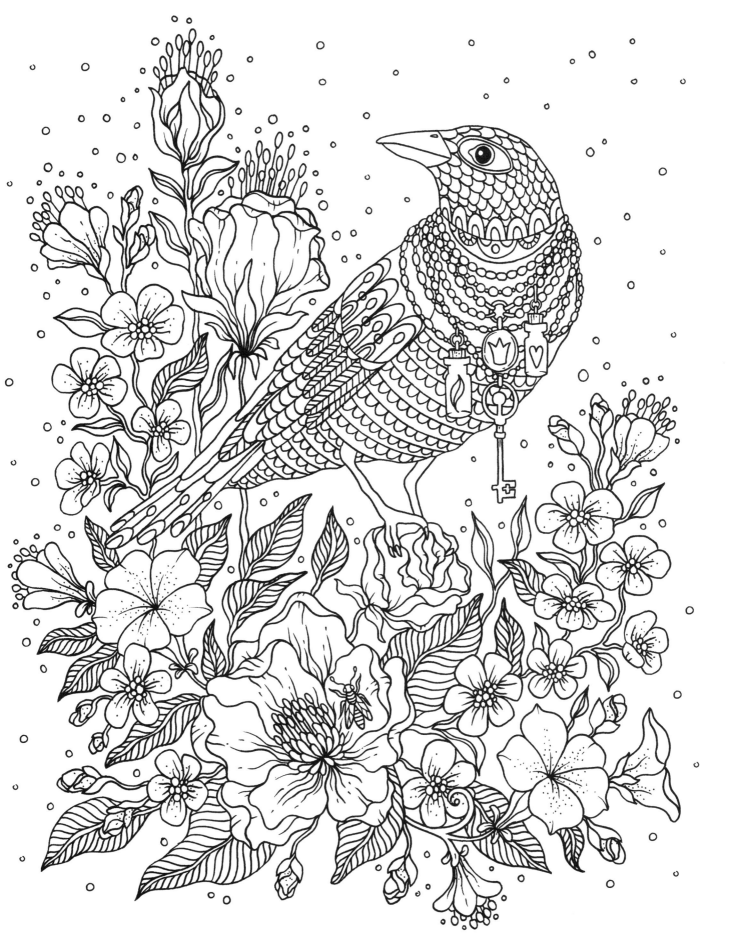

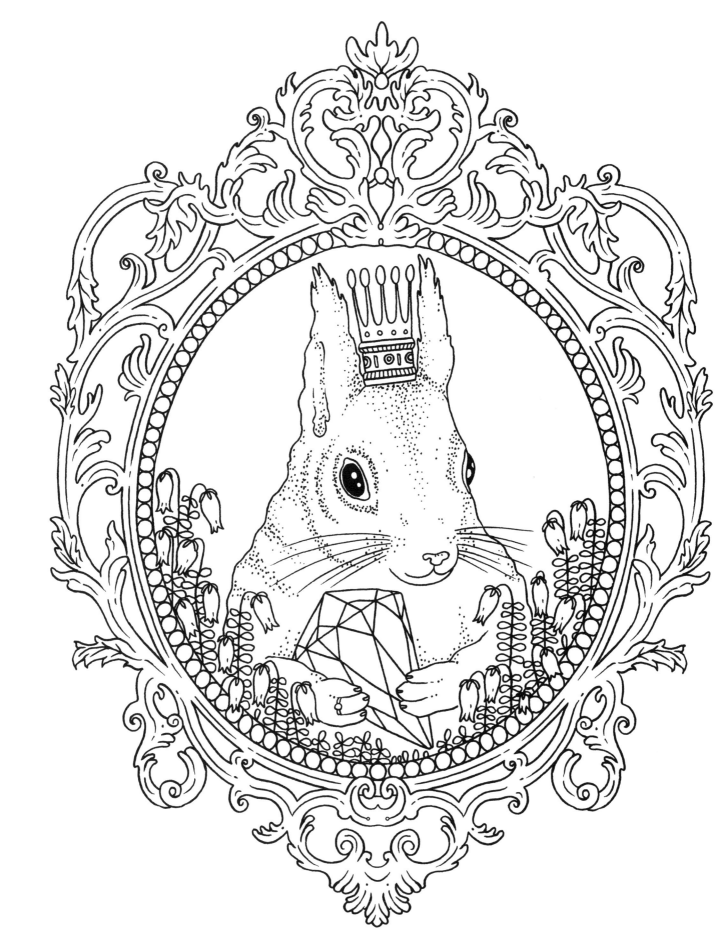

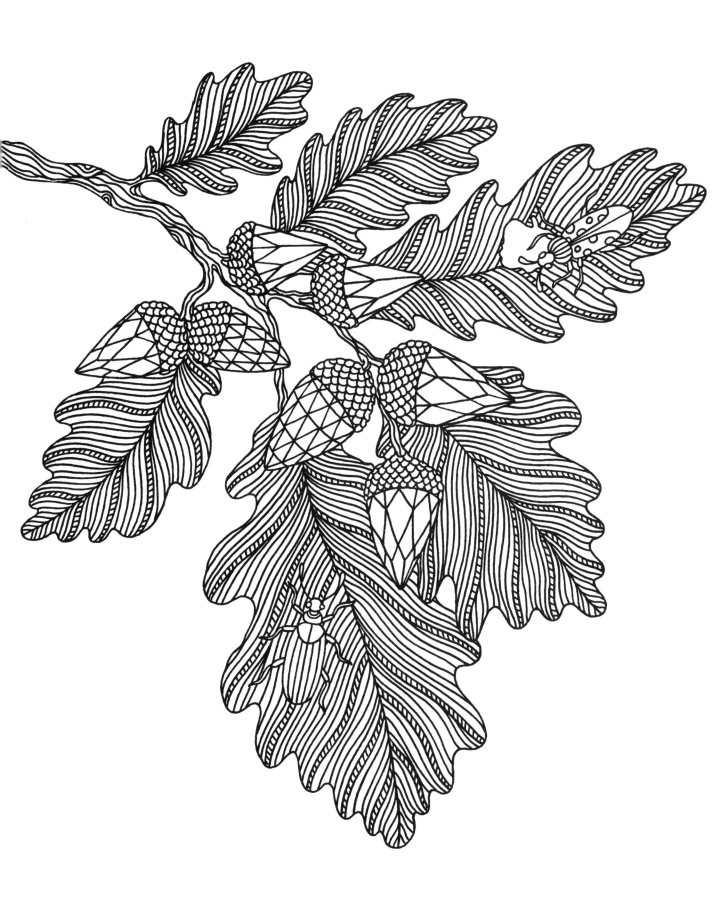

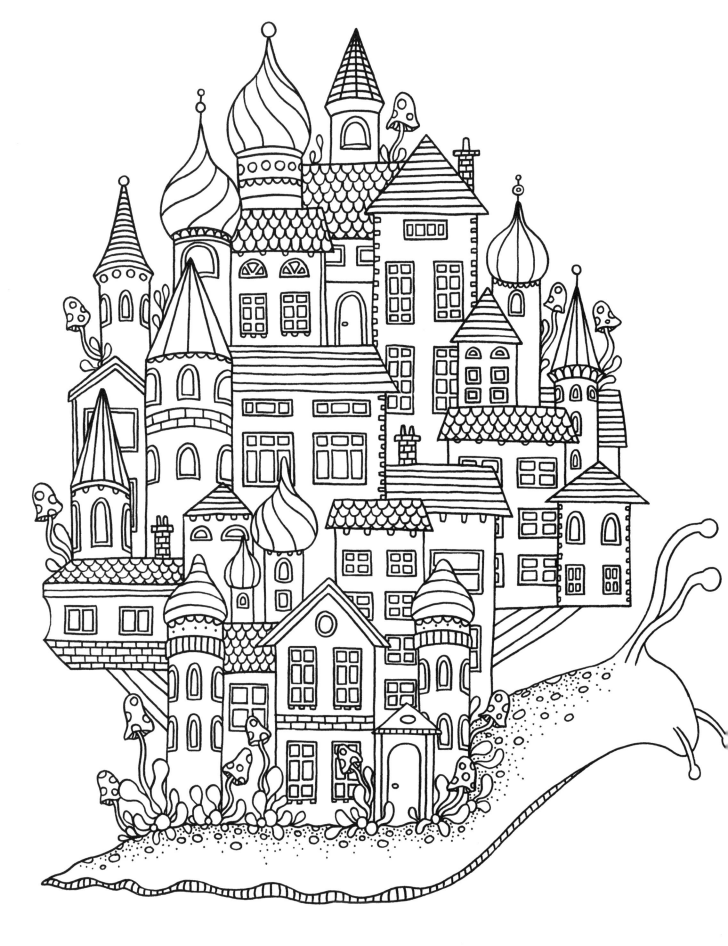

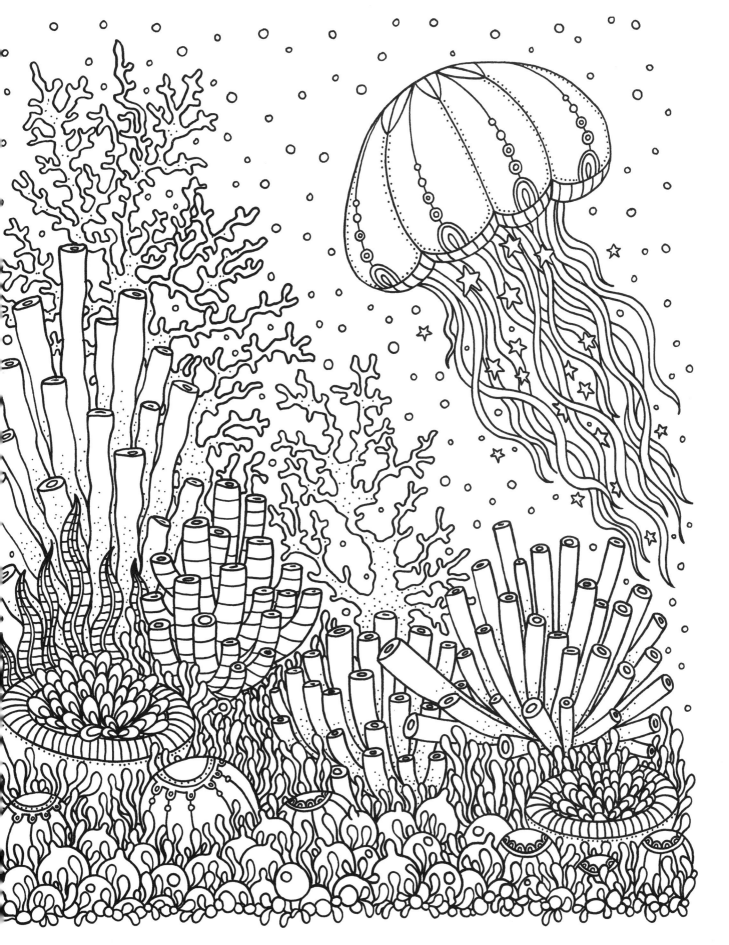

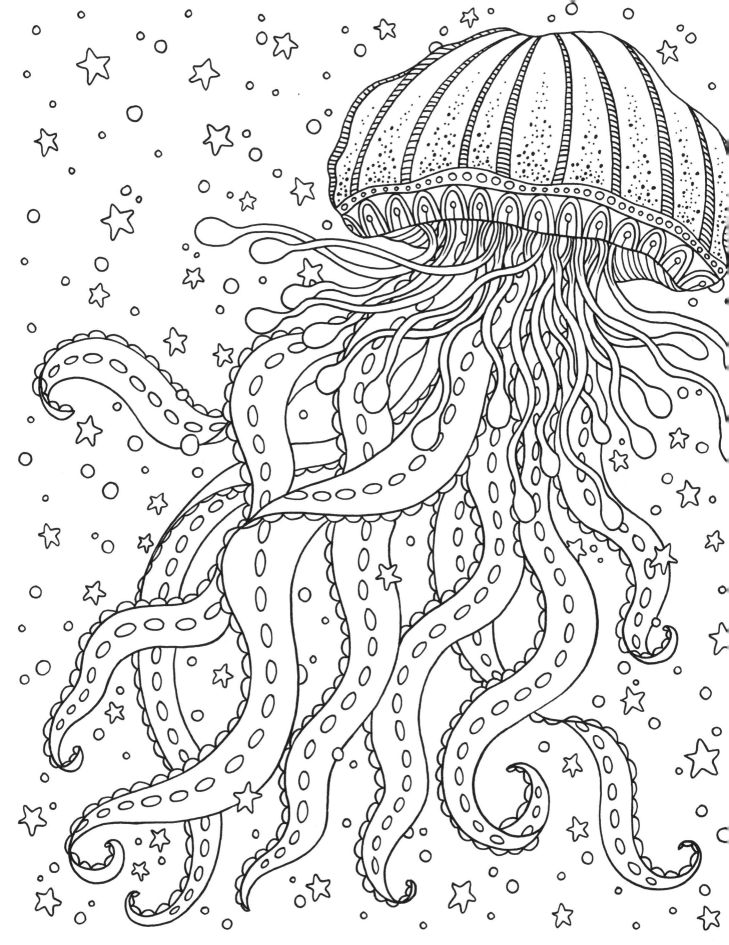

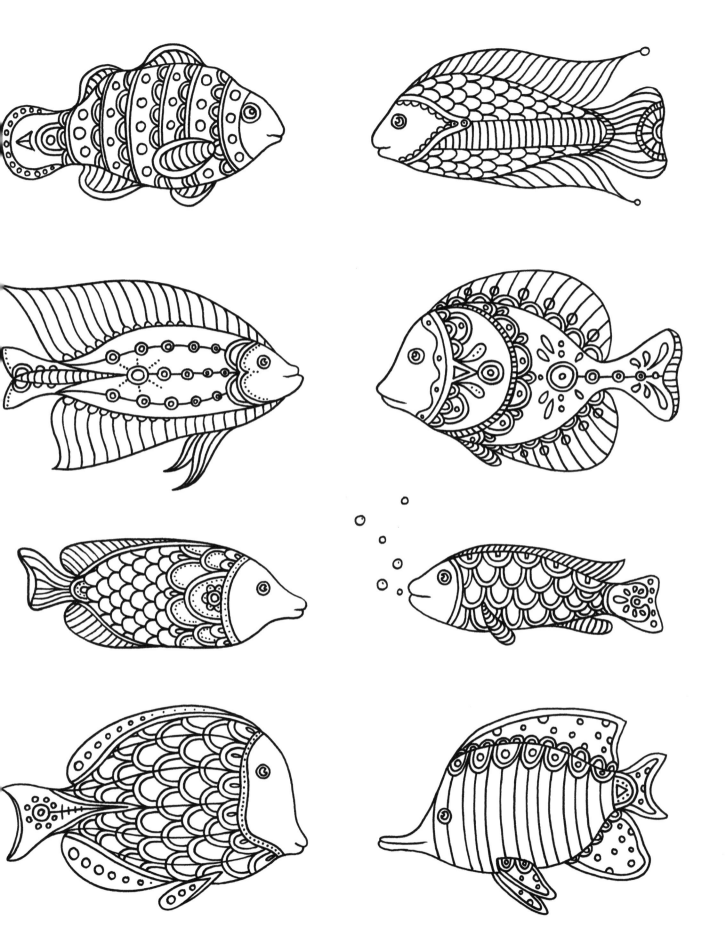

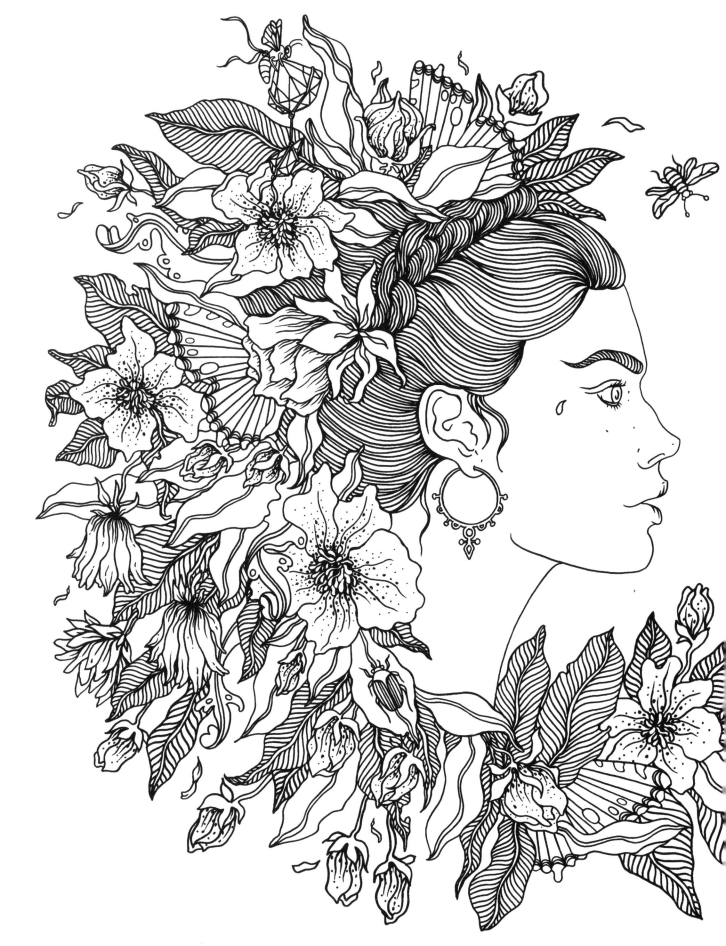

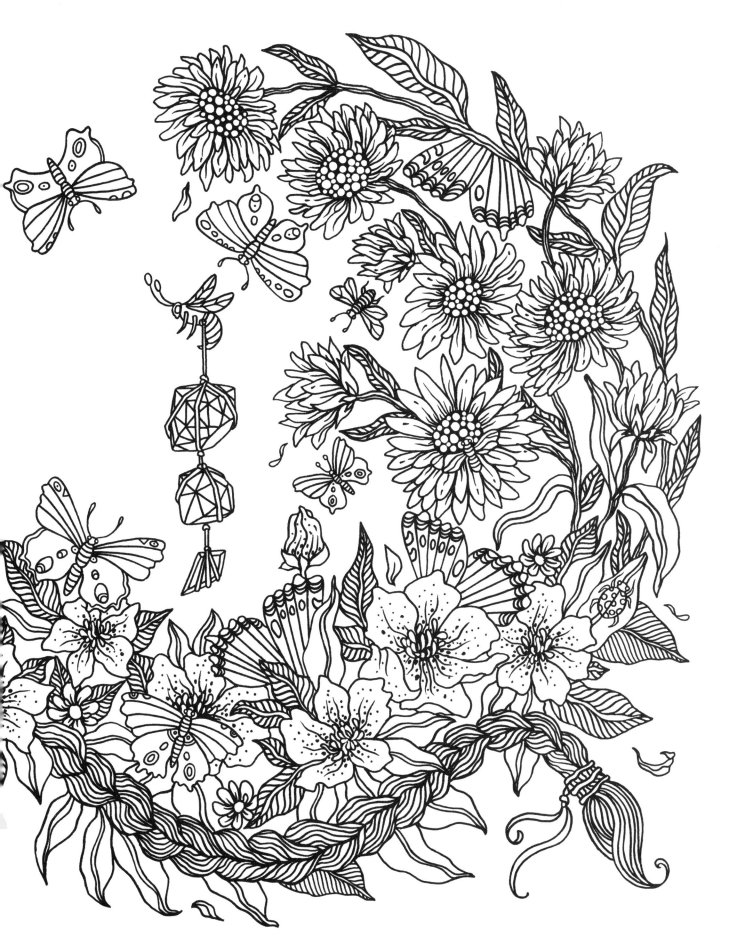

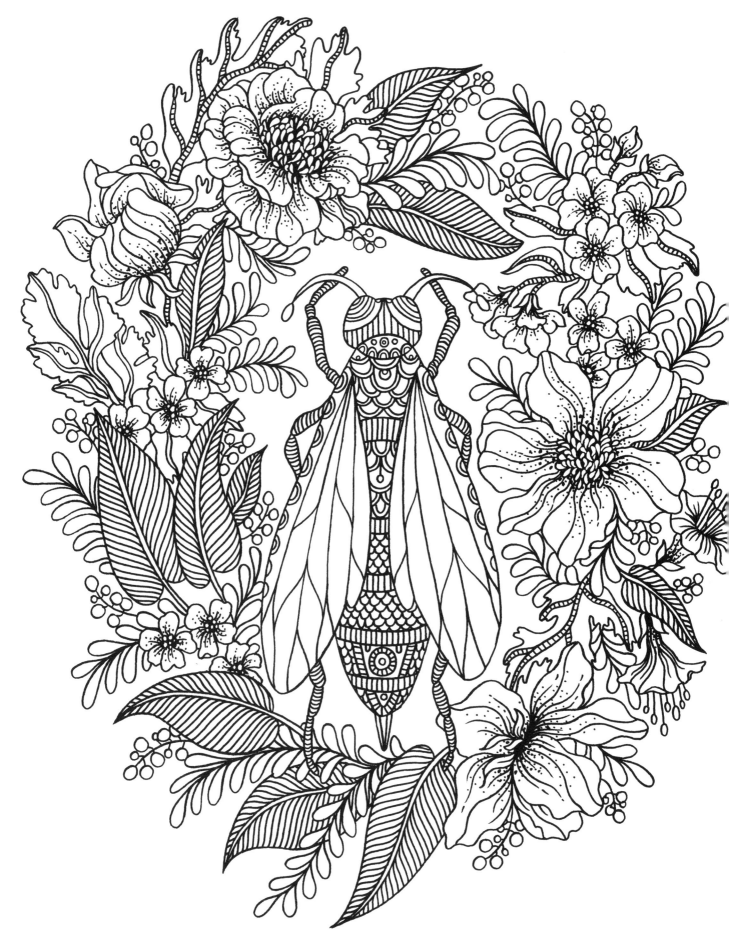

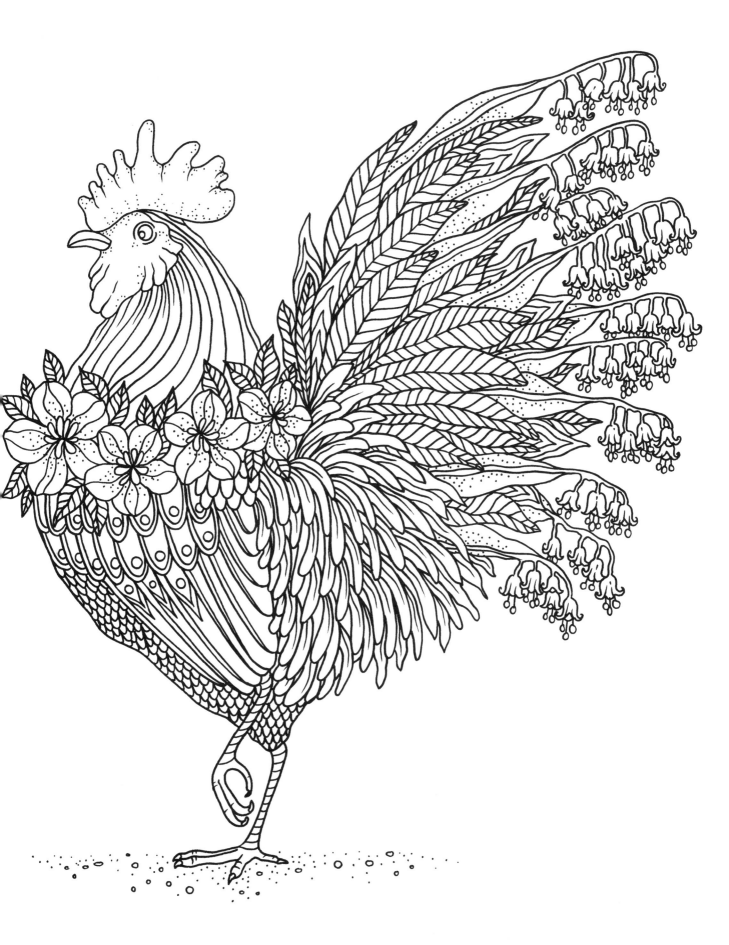

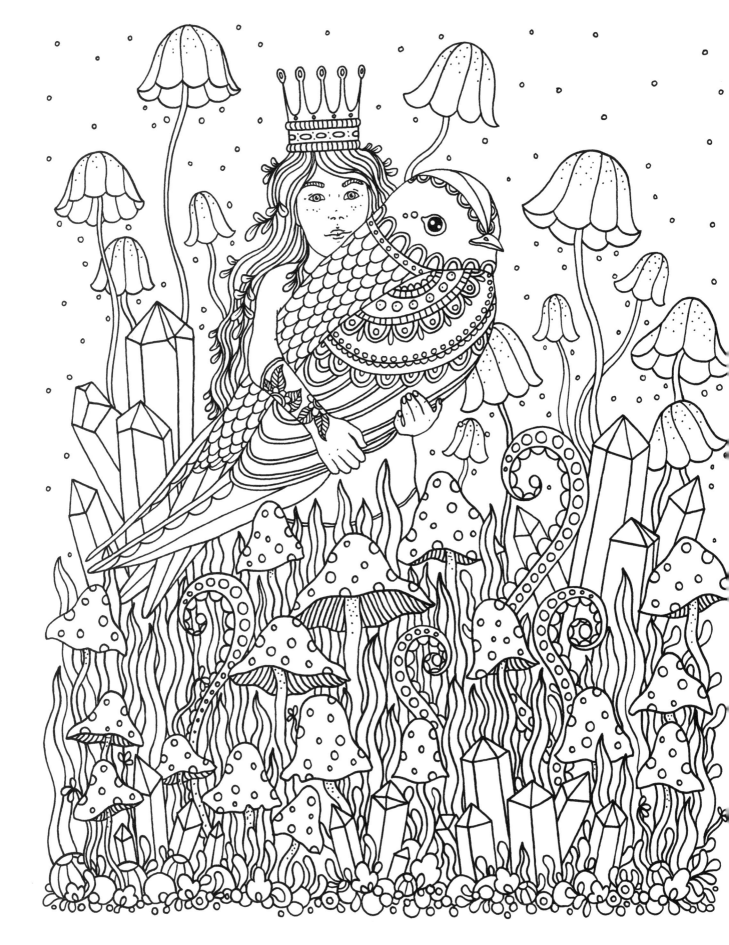

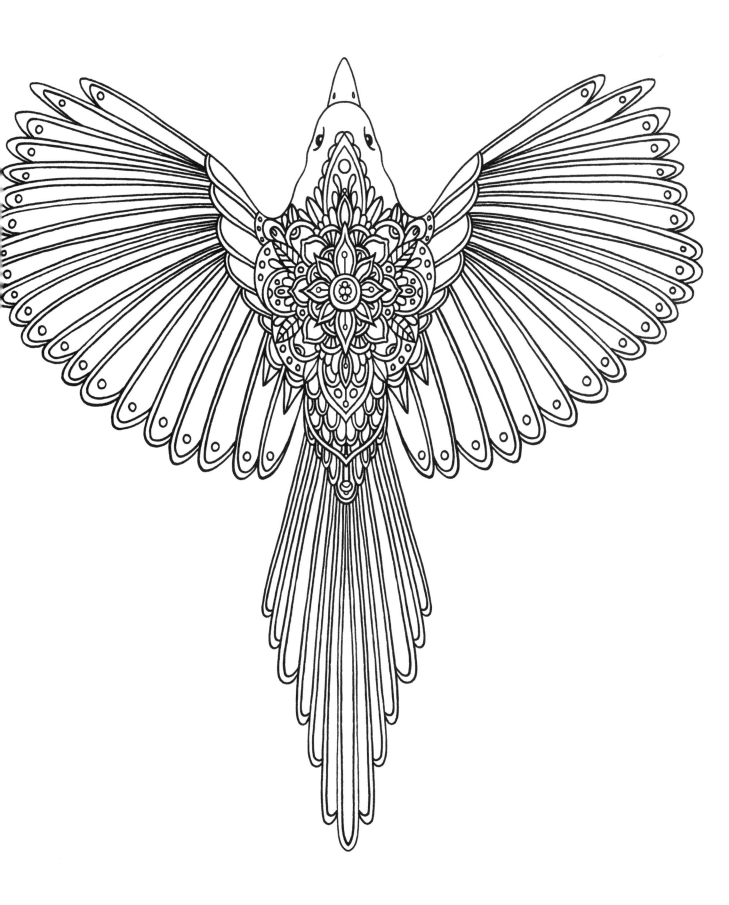

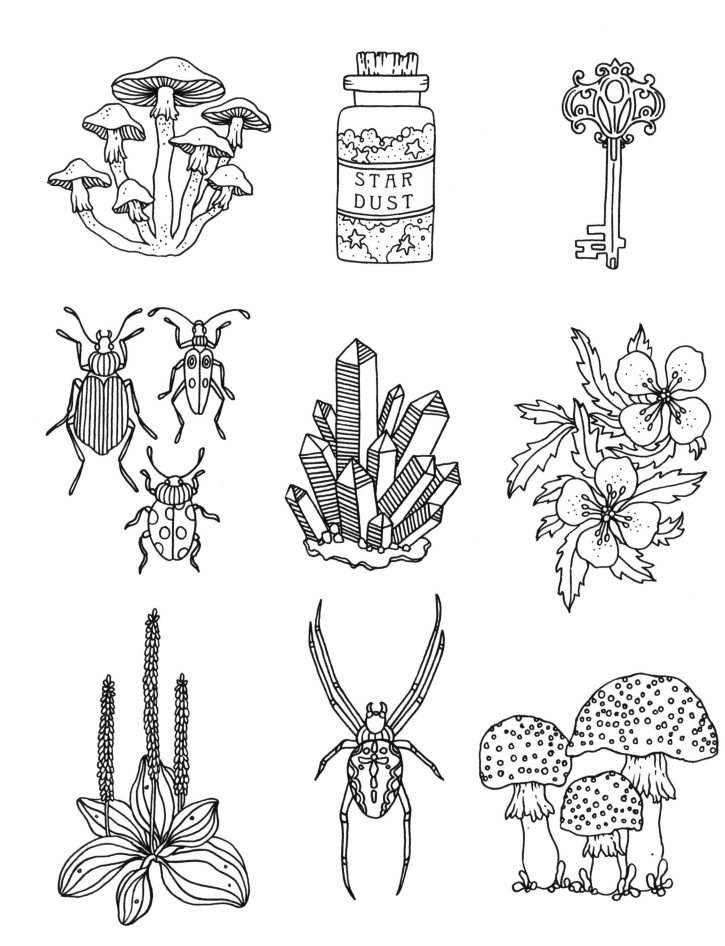

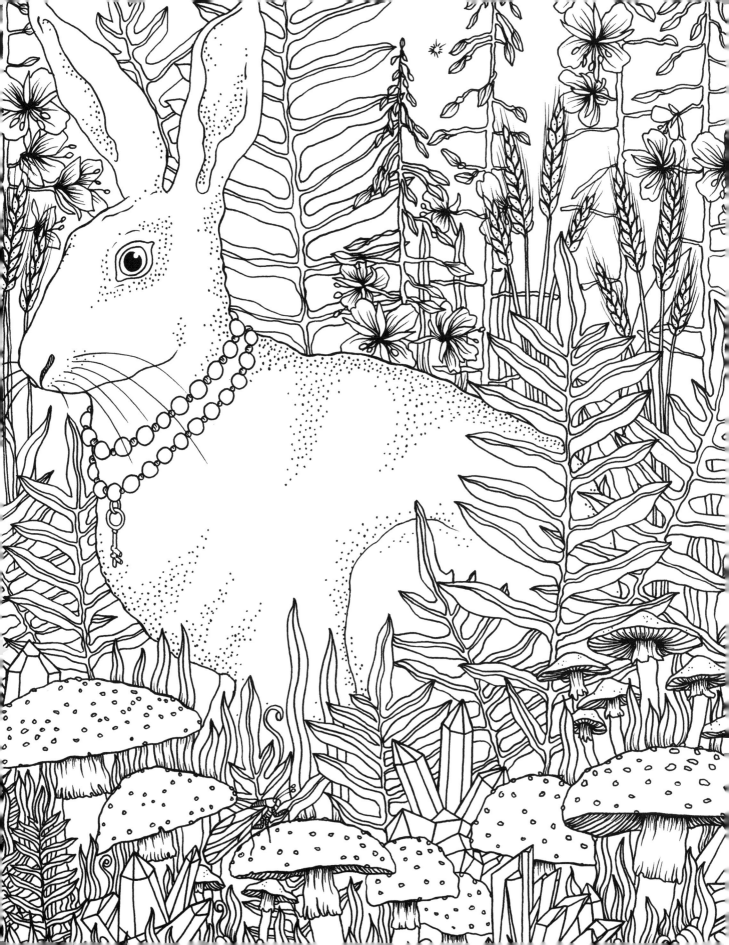

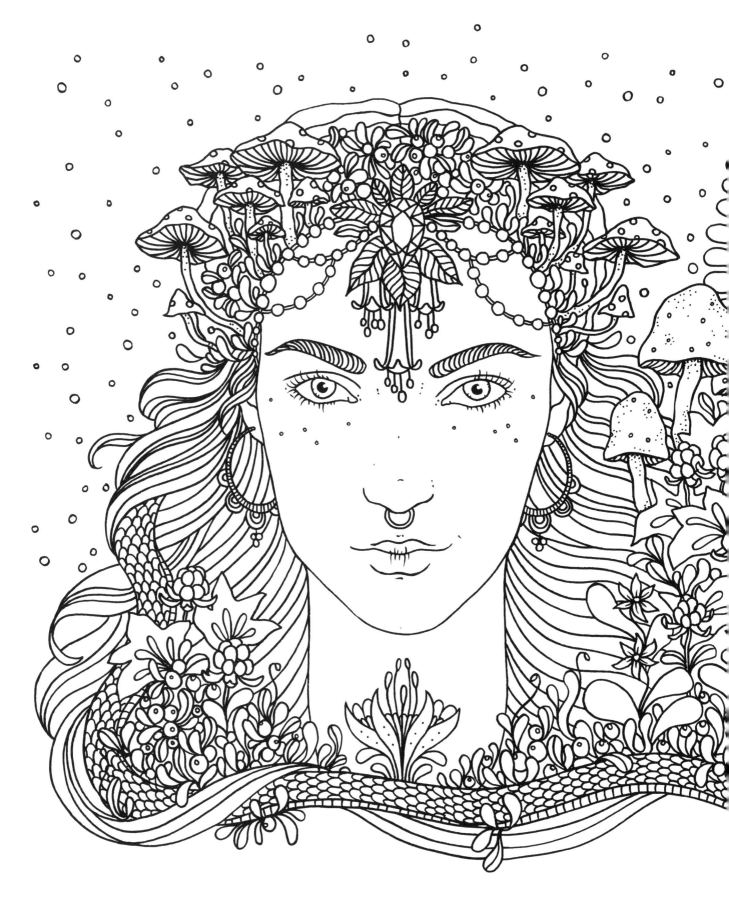

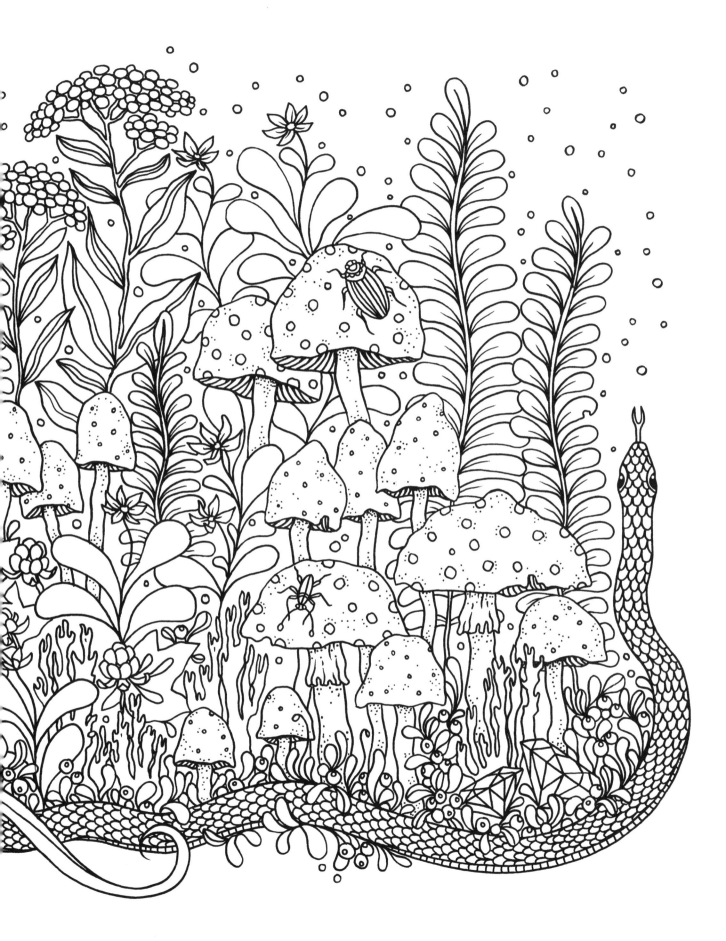

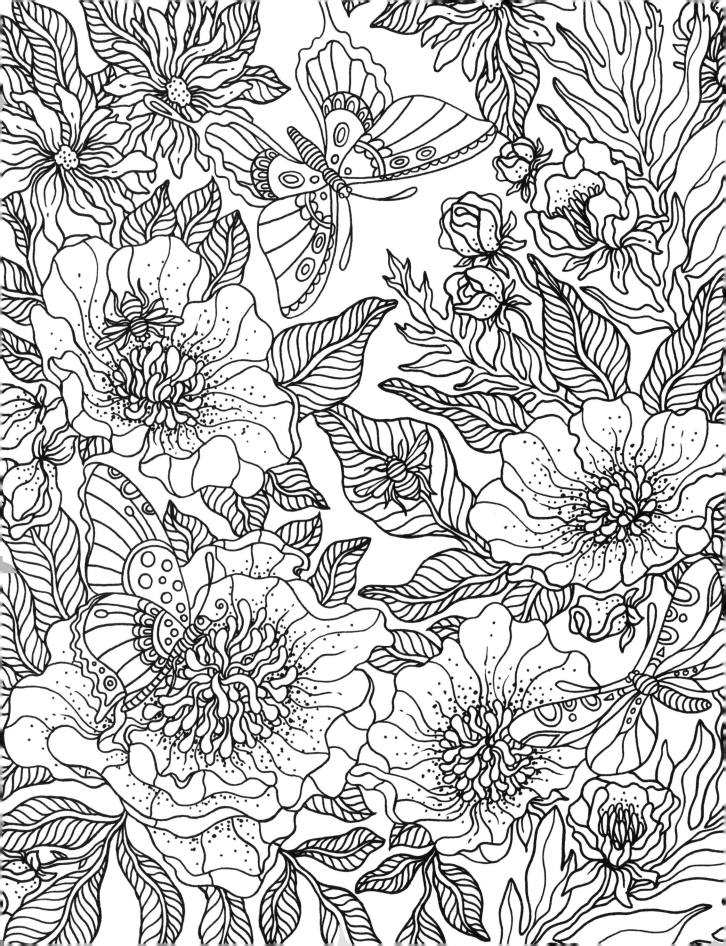

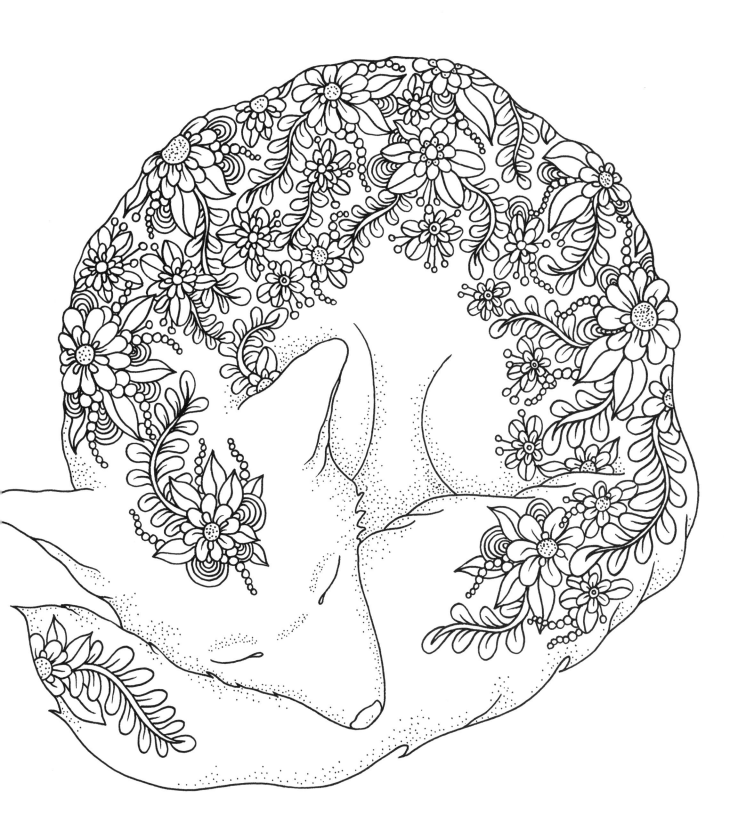

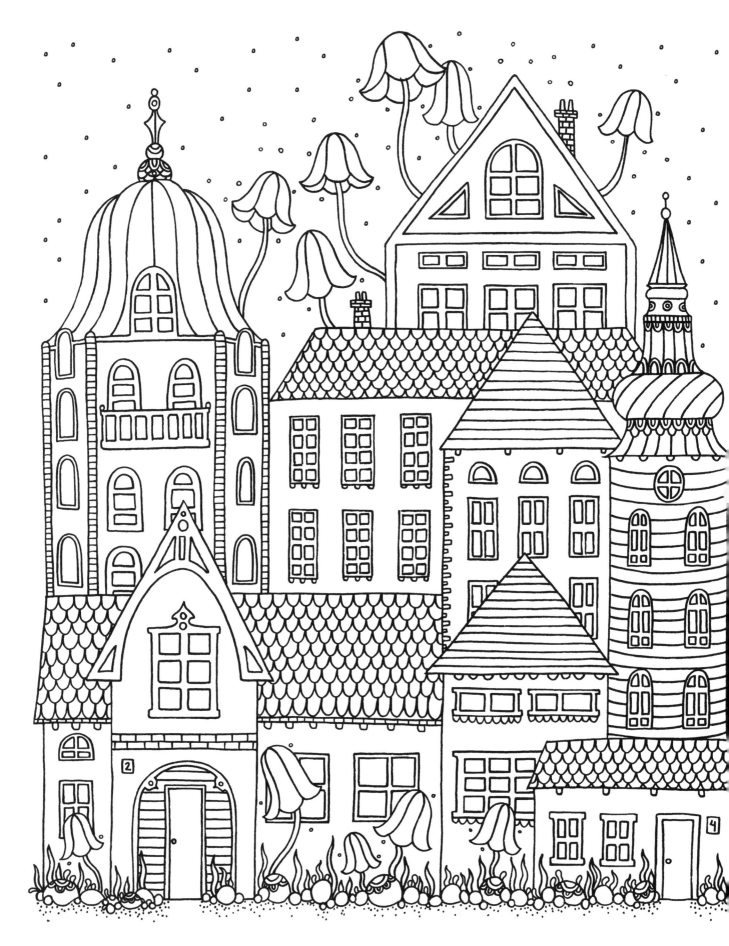

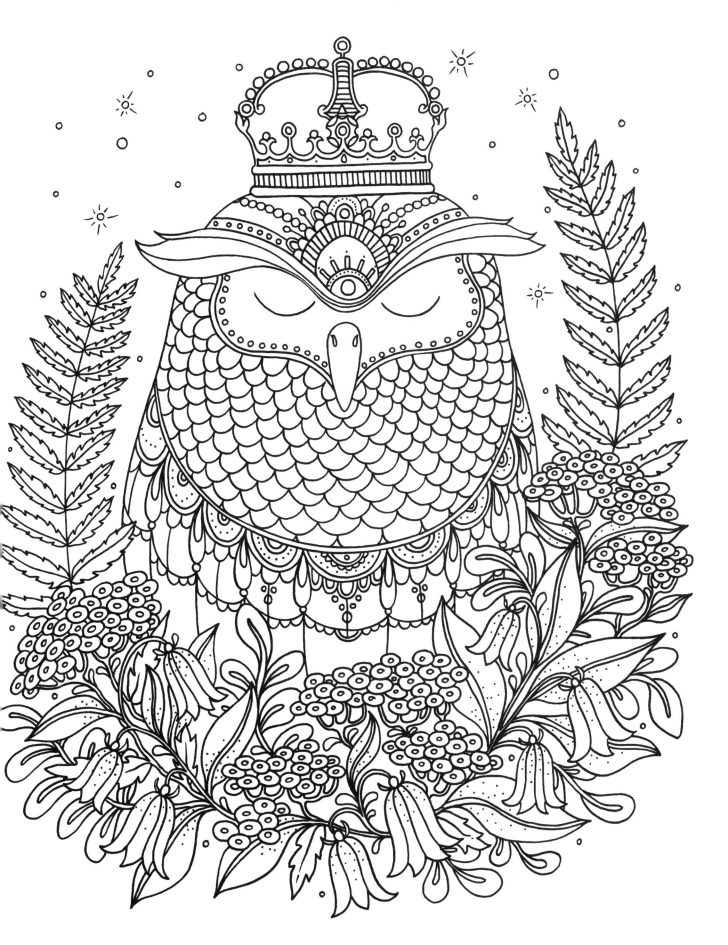

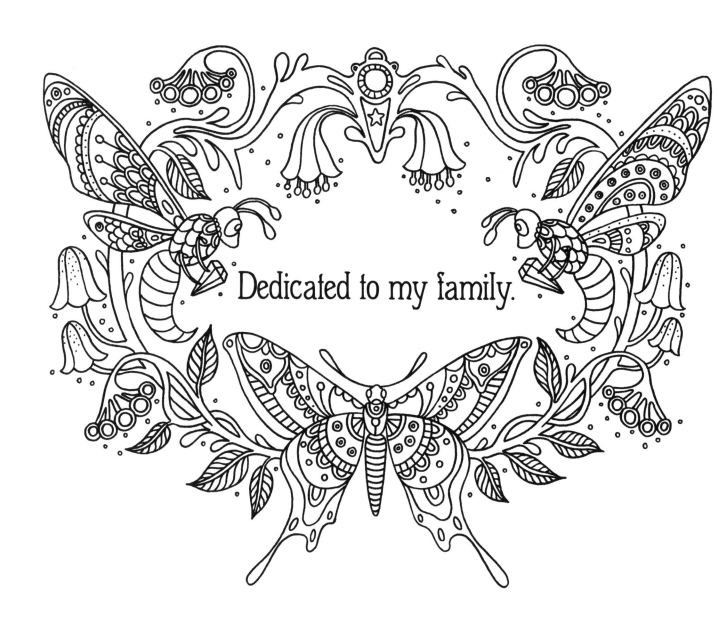

Dedicated to my family.